Www.LarryRedmond.Com

Also by Larry Redmond

A Feast of Peonies (2003)

The Last and Final King (2003)

Satan's Anvil and other stories (2004)

A Lake of Fire (1972, 2006)

The Reward of the Fool (2009)

Why to Kill a Billionaire

Why to Kill a Billionaire

by

Larry Redmond

Penknife Press   Chicago, Illinois

Copyright © 2015 by Larry Redmond
All rights reserved under International and Pan-American Copyright Conventions.
Published in the United States of America by Penknife Press, Ltd., Chicago, Illinois.

ISBN 978-1-59997-033-2

Library of Congress Control Number: 2014960175

Manufactured in the United States of America

Whoever sheds the blood of man, by man shall his blood be shed, for God made man in his own image.

The Holy Bible
Genesis 9:6

. . . because greater is he that is in you, than he that is in the world.

The Holy Bible
1 John 4:4

The lowly will possess the land and will live in peace and prosperity.

The Holy Bible
Psalm 37:11

I

It is a cruel irony that humankind is desperate to know the truth. We want to know the truth about everything. But the truth is elusive, and few, if any, of us have access to it. And when we discover the truth, we feel . . . special. We feel that we have something that other people wish they had. More than money, more than fame, we want the truth.

Once we have what we believe to be the truth, we covet it. We protect it. We guard it against assault. We denounce anything that is contrary to it. As a result, we compete with each other for the right to claim it. Religions compete among themselves for the right to claim that they know the truth. Members of one religion will kill members of other religions in order to demonstrate the strength of their belief in their truth, but also to eliminate competing truths. Christians rally against Muslims. Catholics against Protestants against the Coptics. Shia Muslims against Sunni Muslims. And the Sufis are in there somewhere. There's the Buddhists, the Hindus, the Zoroastrians and, naturally, the atheists all vying for the rightful claim of 'bearer of the truth.'

Science competes with religions making the claim that "myths die hard" when the 'truths' of science are not embraced with the zeal that scientists think they should be.

The problem is that science has fallen short. Science has found the elusive God particle, the particle that was supposed to reveal the truth, confirm that the Standard Model of Particle physics was in fact correct, or confirm that we live in one of multiple universes. But the God particle did neither. With a weight of 126.5 gigaelectronvolts, almost exactly half way between the 115 needed to confirm the Standard Model and the 140 needed to confirm multiple universes, the God particle has revealed nothing. Science is still guessing and spinning the yarn that one day we'll know for sure.

The universe is a burlesque dancer and science is a young man leering from the audience, waiting for her to reveal it all. But she never does and she never will. What science has yet to learn is that what is known won't compensate for what is unknown and unknowable. We cannot extrapolate from what we think we know to what we think we should or could know. Burlesque dancers always conceal the something we most want to see.

It's as if the truth were the Holy Grail. Everybody is looking for it, but nobody seems to be able to grasp more than snippets of it.

Courts of law demand that a witness tell 'the truth, the whole truth, and nothing but the truth,' then proceed to cloud the issue in question with rules and conditions that keep the truth shrouded in confusion, after which the judge will proclaim that 'the truth isn't the truth until I say it's the truth.' What about the real truth, judge?

There was a boxer, Carl Williams, whose moniker was 'the truth.' He had a record of 30 wins, 10 losses and one 'no contest.' One of those losses was against Iron Mike Tyson. Tyson knocked 'the truth' down after 90 seconds of the first round. Several seconds later, the referee stopped the fight. The truth never got a chance to show his stuff.

Lovers demand that they each never lie to the other.

Parents demand the truth from their children, else Santa Claus will bypass their house on Christmas.

Historians routinely claim to finally be revealing the truth about some incident or other, the details of which had been lost in time until now. Who shot Kennedy? Who shot King? All a lot of who-shot-John.

Police officers look for the truth. "Just the facts, ma'am."

Instant replay claims to preserve the truth.

Archeologists dig up the truth.

Government commissions bury the truth. What really did happen to the twin towers or at Waco or at Ruby Ridge?

Or the truth went with whomever to the grave.

Psychiatrists guide their patients in revealing the truth to themselves.

Western philosophers devote countless hours, reams of paper and gallons of ink in explorations of notions that they think will eventually reveal some semblance of the truth. "I think, therefore I am." Thinkers over the years from Socrates and Aristotle to John Locke, Bertrand Russell, Bishop Berkeley, Charles Barkley and Walt Disney have all tried their hand at uncovering the truth. All on some level have failed.

Have aliens really landed?

What really goes on at Area 51?

Mystics have thrown their hats into the quest-for-truth ring. Grigori Rasputin, George Gurdjieff, Edgar Cayce and yogis of all stripes have healed or foretold the future or something that would lead people to believe that they knew the truth. But when pressed for the truth, it all sounded like mumbo-jumbo. Is that what the truth is, mumbo-jumbo gumbo? A little bit of this and a little bit of that? We all hope not. But in fact, nobody really knows for sure.

It is the human condition to desperately yearn for the truth, but never quite find it. The truth, after all, can never truly be known. So what are we doing? Why do we look? Why can't we just live for today content that this moment is all that there is, content that the here-and-now is the only truth in existence to the extent that it is? It's as if the fates are playing a joke on us. We are compelled to search for something that doesn't exist, and therefore cannot be found. It follows that wisdom inheres in ceasing the search. The only truth is that there is no truth. So stop looking for it. The wise man sits back and marvels at the extent of the folly unfolding before him. It's like the man said, "Don't sweat the small shit. And everything is small shit." Small comfort though when what you really want is the truth. And ain't that the truth.

II

On my last job, I had spent nearly a year in Israel. I took round-about flights on my return to the States. I guess I had hoped round-about flights would cover my tracks, but deep down, I knew better. I took a flight to Paris first, then a flight to Stockholm. Both cities served as reminders of the life I had to escape many, many years earlier. Lillian, an older woman– she was about as old then as I was now– I had met years ago while stationed with the Air Force in Germany, who had wanted me to go to Stockholm with her in order to protect me from *Das Innerste Feuer*, a radical religious order that rivaled *Seine Kinder*, another religious order that my great uncle had formed years earlier than that, and that his followers believed I had been destined to resurrect.

Paris was where I had decided that I couldn't be any kind of religious leader, and where I left Lillian in order to return to the States. Both my returns from international travel, the one years ago and this one from Israel, had me apprehensive about my ability to live a normal life.

From Stockholm, I flew to London, then to New York.

After my first return, I spent years living on the streets

of Chicago afraid someone might discover who I was, or rather, who I didn't want to be. My fate upon returning this time was yet to be determined.

My mark, Nathan Benjamin, the prime minister of Israel, was dead. I had killed him, but the Israeli Occupation Force was mounting a massive campaign against the Palestinian territories. The Israeli government had abandoned any pretext of defending itself against the bazooka rockets from Gaza, and now blamed Benjamin's death on the Palestinians. Their plan for Palestinian extermination was completely uncloaked, and they made it crystal clear that they wanted all Palestinian land for Israeli use. It's a plan they had been working on since 1948, but this time they made it sound as if it were brand spanking new. They called it the American model, referring to the extermination of native Americans, and the taking of their land for use by Europeans beginning with the Queen Anne wars.

The Israelis claimed that the security of the entire region required this new aggression. The IOF troops in Gaza and the West Bank were going house to house, room to room, killing anything that moved, men, women and children. The Zionists learned much during their tenure in Germany. And to prevent the Palestinian injured from being adequately treated, the IOF bombed hospitals and all the surrounding infrastructure.

Their plan was timed to coincide with the unrest sweeping the Arab world. While Arab governments were busy dealing with the push for democracy in their respective countries, the Israelis mounted their attack. I think they thought the Middle East was up for grabs, and they wanted to get theirs while the getting was good.

I felt for the Palestinians, but I had to do what I had to do. Benjamin was the third Antichrist, and he had to be stopped. I stopped him, but I was no longer sure I had stopped him in time. Maybe the world would still erupt into war because of what Benjamin had already done. Unwittingly, I may have furthered the prophecy. Maybe I should have let him live.

It hadn't, after all, been easy to kill him. I tracked his comings and goings for months before I discovered a loose pattern. I discovered that on those days when he addressed the Knesset, he always had his security people with him. I decided to try to reach one of them.

It took a while. Months as a matter of fact. But I finally managed to find a woman whose allegiance was more to money than to her country. She was a little slip of a thing, barely a hundred pounds, with tits like fried eggs and eyes to match. But she was strictly business.

"It's going to cost you," she told me.

"How much?" I asked.

She told me her price, and I told her no problem.

She knew where one of his security people liked to hang out when he wasn't on duty, some little club on the strip in Jerusalem. She confided that he had once been one of her best customers, but that his sights had been turned by a younger, newer purveyor of the services he enjoyed. I didn't tell her this, but I figured that her working with me was her way of getting even with the bastard.

The plan was to accidentally-on-purpose bump into him at this club, then she would introduce me as her new *beau*. It worked better than either of us had expected.

"I've seen you around here before," he said to me upon my being introduced. Then he asked, "How long have you known Ariella?"

He was tall and angular like an athlete. I suppose that was part of the job. Dirty blond hair, puppy brown eyes. He had a dimple in his chin, and there was a pimple on one side of it.

I was sitting at the bar drinking a gin and tonic *sans* the gin with a squeeze of lemon and a squeeze of lime. Ariella had made her way over to a corner where she was chatting up some other women whom I guessed were business colleagues.

"This is my first time here," I responded.

"But I have seen you," he said. He ordered a Bloody Mary *sans* the vodka.

I began to wonder if he had seen me on surveillance tapes as I had been tracking Benjamin. I tried to misdirect him.

"I'm relatively new in town," I said.

"Where you from?" he asked.

"New York," I lied.

"Manhattan?" he asked.

"Mt. Vernon," I lied again.

"I love New York," he said. "I went to school there."

"What did you study?"

"Law and international relations," he answered. "I needed both degrees for my current job."

Now I was worried. I knew what his job was. And if he was telling me the truth, it meant I was in grave danger. It meant that I had been compromised somehow. I tried to remain cool.

"What do you do?" I asked.

"I studied at New York University," he said. "Great school."

I didn't want to show it, but I was beginning to feel

like a mouse in a game of cat and mouse. I began re-examining the months I had spent trying to get a handle on Benjamin's routine. Had I been careless, reckless? Had I gotten too close? At the same time I was going over my reconnoiter regiment, I began watching him more closely. I couldn't take the chance that he wouldn't try something heroic, like slipping something into my drink, or maybe even launching a physical attack on my person.

"So what do *you* do?" he asked.

I always keep a cover story handy. My passport was in my latest name, so I didn't have to worry about remembering how I should answer.

"I'm a freelance photographer," I answered, "working on getting some pictures for a couple of travel magazines I submit to."

"Got any images handy?" he asked.

"Not here," I answered. Then I asked, "Why? Do you take pictures, too?"

"I love taking pictures," he answered. "And I love looking at them."

I was beginning to feel relaxed in our conversation. That's when I knew I had to keep my guard up. If he were planning something, he would want me to be relaxed and off guard. I decided it was time to make my exit.

"Look," I said, finishing my tonic water, "I've got a busy day tomorrow. I've got to turn it."

I turned my glass up to get the last swallow. I couldn't shake the feeling that I hadn't been the stalker here. I had wanted to meet one of Benjamin's men, but somehow, this meeting wasn't my doing at all. It was his. *He* had been stalking *me*. Maybe he had sent Ariella to me in order for her to bring me to him. And that had me worried, because I was supposed to be invisible.

"Take my number," he said. "I'd like to see some of your work."

He gave me a card with his number scribbled on the back.

"That's my cell," he said. "Maybe we can have lunch or something."

"Sure," I lied. "Maybe tomorrow."

"My name is Menachem," he said.

I set my glass down, hailed Ariella and headed for the door. I couldn't just leave her there. That would look too suspicious. And I didn't want to have to turn my back to him, but I took the chance. Once outside, I turned the corner, and almost ran to the nearest taxi stand pulling Ariella behind me, her little legs barely keeping up. My first thought as the taxi pulled away from the curb was that I had to leave the country, and fast.

"What is the matter with you?" she asked.

I didn't know what to answer. Maybe I was wrong. Maybe she *wasn't* working for him.

"Here's the rest of the money I owe you," I said, passing her a sealed envelop.

She opened the envelop on the spot and counted it all out. "It's all here," she said. "You can let me out on the next corner."

With Ariella gone, I could concentrate on my next move. I gave the driver my address. I had it written down on a card so I wouldn't have to worry about my pronunciation. He looked at me in the rearview mirror, and nodded. I wondered when the next plane left for anyplace in Europe. We pulled up to my building, and I passed money to the driver, but he refused to take it.

"Here," I said, "take this. Take it all. I won't be needing it."

Instead of taking the money, he got out and opened my door for me. He was short, barely five feet. He had a sunken, shriveled face that was leathery, as if he had made his living working for decades in the sun. As he opened the door, one of those minivan sliding doors, he had this beatific smile on his face. His expression was one that you might expect to see on an elf, if there were elves. His eyes almost twinkled. He wore a beret, and he pulled it off as I exited.

"I know who you are," he said in perfect English. Then he hopped back into his taxi, and pulled away from the curb. "My name is Yohanan," he shouted back at me through the open window.

Clearly, my cover was blown. I had to get to the airport tonight.

In my room, I began packing my bag to leave. I was staying with a couple of Congolese exchange students I had met my first week in town. They were now out of town on a holiday, so I had the flat to myself. I didn't know whether or not my roommates were typical Congolese, but they had posters of Patrice Lumumba posted all over the place along with posters of Malcolm X. They claimed that both Lumumba and Malcolm were victims of CIA assassinations.

They claimed Lumumba, the first democratically elected prime minister of the Republic of the Congo, was murdered in order for the U.S. puppet, Mobutu Sese Seko, to kill democracy in his own country, which he did, and give U.S. corporations unfettered access to mineral resources in the Congo, which he did. They claimed that the U.S. was using that same tactic around the world, especially in Africa and Latin America. Anywhere in the world that people had established a democratic form of government, the U.S. destroyed it, and installed a puppet who catered to the whims of corporate interests.

They insisted the CIA killed Malcolm in order to thwart the Black nationalist movement in America. I knew they were right, but I couldn't afford to get sidetracked. I was here on a mission.

I packed quickly and quietly. I couldn't have been there more than fifteen minutes when someone knocked at the front door. Thinking it was one of my roommates returning, I opened to door hastily. I wanted to get back to my packing so I could get out of Dodge. It was Menachem.

"We need to talk," he said. He walked in uninvited. I began looking around the room for things he might try to use as weapons.

I knew the answer, but I asked the question anyway. "How did you find me here?"

"That's not important," he answered. "What's important is that I did find you."

I cut right to the chase. "Why were you looking?"

"That's the wrong question again," he countered. "The

right question is what are *you* looking for?"

"You seem to have all the answers," I said. "So you tell me."

He paused for a moment. Then he said, "Israel is in big trouble."

"And how do I fit into that?" I asked.

"The country I love is about to be destroyed," he continued, ignoring my question.

Maybe I had asked the wrong question again.

"Have you seen our Supreme Court Building?" he asked.

"No," I answered.

"You should. It's an architectural marvel."

"I'm not much into architecture."

"No matter," he said. "It's the math that makes the building marvelous, not the architecture, *per se*."

"Cut to the chase," I urged.

He paused a moment, then said, "There are remarkable similarities between the architecture here in Jerusalem and that in Washington, D.C."

"So what's your point?"

"My point is this. The same people who built Washington built our capital."

"And?"

"The same people who run the government here run

the government there."

"Washington, D.C., was designed hundreds of years ago."

"Yes, I know," he said. "Which means somebody, some group of people is affecting the direction of humanity over time. And they are affecting it in a way that does not benefit humanity, but rather benefits the group doing the affecting."

That struck a chord. I recalled a conversation I had months earlier with . . .. Who was it? Then I recalled his image. He was a big man, six foot six, two hundred and fifty pounds. His hairline formed an "M" over his high and broad forehead. His name was Reverend Milton, and the question I asked him back then was, who's giving the orders that seem to end as plans to poison Black people generation after generation after generation? But Milton didn't know. And he was ashamed of not knowing, because he had spent years trying to figure it out.

I recalled his booming voice saying, "The plan is masterful. The formulators of the plan put rules into place for the common man to follow, because as long as he is busy following the rules, he won't even conceive of the notion that there is a plan in place, a plan that he ain't part of. The United States Constitution was put into place to give the people the illusion that they are masters of their own destiny. An elaborate system of government was created with seeming checks and balances, with seeming recourse for injustices, with seeming rules for the way the country is run. But it's a fake. It's all a fake. Oh, it works on a certain low level. And the working on that level helps perpetuate the fiction that it works on all levels. It helps perpetuate the fiction that there is no master plan in place. That's part of the beauty of the plan. As people see the every day workings of government, they begin to believe what they see. After a while, when evidence of how things really work surfaces— briberies, stolen elections, political favors, cronyism, assassinations— the people see *them* as abnormalities, aberrations."

It took me a moment to recover from my reverie. When I did, I looked at Menachem, and asked, "So who might this group of people be?"

"The Masons," he said. He didn't even have to think about it.

"The *Free*masons?!" I was stunned. "The Ancient *Free* and *Accepted* Masons?! Heros of the universe?! Knights Templar and all that shit?!"

"Yes," he answered.

"That cannot be," I said. "I know folks who are

Masons. They help folks. They raise money for children."

"They instigate wars, and feed on mankind," he countered. "People forget that it was the Masons through their military arm, the Knights Templar, who started the Crusades. It gets romanticized in Western culture by claiming they were seeking the whereabouts of the Holy Grail. But their true mission was the eradication of Islam from the face of the earth. But they failed. They were beaten back and eventually destroyed.

"These days, the Masons control the governments of Israel and the United States, and use the armed forces of those countries to do what the Knights Templar could not. That's what the war on terror is *really* about, the eradication of Islam from the planet. And the folks you know who are Masons don't know shit about what the Masons are really about."

Maybe he had a point. Everybody I knew who was a Mason joined in order to get their traffic tickets fixed. They would stand before the judge with their heels together and their feet at right angles relating some tale about being a traveler on the square, and the judge would know what that meant, and let them off. I never believed it. But then again, I never tried it.

"So what is this architecture shit about?"

"Do you know what the Washington Monument is?"

Of course I knew. It was an Egyptian obelisk. But I wanted to know what *he* thought it was. So I played the nut role.

"No," I said, "what is it?"

"It is the symbol of the Antichrist. And there is one just like it here in Jerusalem."

My heart quickened. It made no sense, but I had clearly found the right person. It was as if Ida's crazy everything-is-everything randomness about the universe was proving to be right. I needed for Menachem to tell me more.

III

When I was a kid, we used to say that the Devil was beating his wife whenever it rained while the sun shone. I would have images of Him standing belt in hand over some sweet, innocent damsel. She would be crying; He would be laughing. It never crossed my young mind that she couldn't have been so sweet or innocent if she was the Devil's wife. She was, after all, the Devil's wife, and, hence, consigned to hell. And it certainly never crossed my mind that maybe He was beating her because she wanted to be beaten. That juxtaposition of the words, 'wanted to be beaten,' simply did not compute. I was good and grown before I was introduced to the notion that, indeed, there were people in the world who 'wanted to be beaten,' who got off on it, who sought it at every turn.

By good and grown, I meant a short while after my return trip from Israel. That's when I met Brit. I had been working on my photography skills, and covering one of the Dump Walker rallies in Madison, Wisconsin. She was up there covering the rally for some left-wing newspaper with a circulation of about a thousand.

I was on the third level of the rotunda getting a wide-angle shot of the crowd. It was a great shot! I had an 80 to 16 millimeter zoom lens pulled all the way back to the 16 millimeter slot on a ten megapixel camera with a top-mounted flash. The shot captured the people with their signs, pink and white with red and black lettering, on the third level across the rotunda as well as the protesters clad in their blue denim pants and red ponchos and sweatshirts surrounding the railing on the circular balcony on the second level that looked down on the revelers and their signs calling on the lower lever for the recall of Governor Walker. I had captured the mood of the rally in that one frame.

"I need a copy of that picture," she said as I turned around to examine the image I had just taken. "Can I see it?"

She was a big woman, tall and heavy. She wore a big, green, down parka and what looked like black, ranger combat boots. She had a tablet on a clipboard. The tablet had lots of scribbles. She was a sister with dark, silky skin like dark chocolate. She had a broad face with a wide nose and thick lips. Her eyes were a deep brown, and her glance wandered back and forth as if she were always looking for something. She had a mole just over the outside of her left eyebrow.

"Sure," I answered, and angled the back of the camera in her direction.

"Yeah," she said, "I need a copy of that. I like the way you got that gold molding atop the green marble columns. I'll pay you for it."

She gave me her card, and went on about the business of interviewing local union members. She was strictly professional.

When I got back to Chicago, I sent her an e-mail telling her the picture was ready. I wanted to send it as an attachment, but she wanted a hard copy. I printed it out, and sent for her address. She wanted to meet for coffee. When I told her that I wasn't based in Madison, rather in Chicago, she suggested that we meet at the Starbuck's café over on 71st and Stony Island Avenue.

"You do nice work," she said, blowing into a cup of tea in order to cool it enough to sip.

"So what's this paper you work for?" I asked.

"It's not really a paper," she answered. "I do an on-line political blog that about a thousand people follow."

"So why don't you take your own pictures?"

"I usually do."

"But you didn't have a wide-angle lens for the rotunda shot?"

"Yeah," she answered, "I had one."

"So why use mine?"

"I'm not going to."

"So why are we here?"

"We're here to talk."

"About what?"

"Oh, you're a big boy now. I'm sure you'll figure it out."

Well, apparently I didn't figure it out, because we talked about photography and art and politics and world events for about an hour.

Then she asked if I had any pain medication on me, because she had a headache. I didn't, and told her as much. She lamented that she hated having to deal with the pain.

Out of the blue, she asked, "So, how are *you* at handling pain?"

I thought it was an odd question, but I answered, "I don't get headaches often."

"I mean, how are you at inflicting it?" Her gaze was fixed on her cup of tea.

"I know how to hurt people." I didn't want to tell her that I knew how to kill people. But again, I guess I missed the real point of her query.

"How are you at inflicting pain for pleasure?"

"Is there such a thing?" I asked.

She looked at me, made that sucking sound with her tongue that people make when they are disappointed or disgusted, then looked back down at her tea.

"How old are you?" she asked.

I told her.

"You're a bit old to not know this shit."

"What shit?"

"I guess I'm going to have to teach you," she said.

It had been a long time since I had been with a woman who treated me like a child, but it seemed as if all the women in my life ended up teaching me something. I recalled my first episode with Ruby many years ago. She was the one who introduced me to sex.

I had just graduated from high school, and I was still a virgin. She invited me to a party at her house. As the evening progressed, we found ourselves alone in one of her bedrooms. One thing led to another until she finally led me to feeling her naked crouch for several minutes before her mother came in and caught us. She was the first woman whose pussy I had ever touched.

Actually, Ruby had been the second woman whose pussy I had touched. The first had been Miss Abbey when I was a child. The point is, though, it was she who had initiated it. She taught me, because I didn't know shit about women or how to become intimate with them. And thinking about it, the same thing was true of Miss Abbey. Even as a child, women were teaching me things about their bodies.

"I'm going to have to teach you about the birds and the bees," Brit said.

"What?" I wasn't sure we were talking about the same thing at all.

After Ruby, there was Frieda. Frieda was the one who taught me about breaking the rules, about having girlfriends on the side. And again, it was she who had initiated our affair.

All of a sudden, I could see Frieda again the day she was killed, blood still wet on her nose and lips and teeth, her eyes half closed and focused on nothing. I blinked my eyes and shook my head to dislodge the image.

"About the birds and bees," Brit said again.

She paused for a long moment.

"Do you know what a sub is?"

"Somehow," I said, "I get the impression you're not talking about boats or sandwiches."

"Nor yet substitute teachers," she quipped.

There was something in her tone that reminded me of Amelia, a little emotionally disturbed white girl I fucked with abandon when I was married to Ida. Brit and Amelia had nothing in common that I knew about, but still some resemblance was clear, at least in my head.

I tried to recall what, if anything, Amelia had taught

me. I drew a blank. All I could remember was the plaintive tone in her voice as she moaned another man's name while looking at me. "Please don't leave me, Melvin," she had said.

"So what are we talking about?" I asked Brit.

"Me," she said.

"You're a sub?" I clearly had no idea what she meant.

"Yes," she answered.

"Okay," I said, "Teach. What the fuck is a sub?"

I felt as if I were asking the question in jest. I mean, how could she possibly come up with a definition of sub that I didn't know? My surprise at her answer was genuine.

"I like playing mind games where there is a transfer of power," she said.

"What do you mean by that?" I saw images of electrons whirling around spinning protons.

"I mean that I give you, for a limited time and within defined limits, the power to control me."

"You mean," I hesitated, "you will do anything I tell you to do?" The whirling electrons and protons vanished.

"Yes," she answered. Her gaze into my eyes did not waver. "You will have complete power over me."

"So I can make you wash dishes."

"Yes."

"I can make you," I hesitated again, "take your clothes off."

"Yes."

"But you hardly know me."

"Oh, that's part of the excitement. I love being intimate with strangers."

"That's dangerous," I replied. "Someone could get hurt doing that."

"Yes," she answered, "and sometimes they do."

I thought about it for a moment. I was in way over my head, but I was intrigued. I began to wonder how far I could go with her. So I asked.

"How far can I take this?"

"That's the part we negotiate," she said.

"Are you going to ask me for money?"

"No, honey. I am not a postitute."

"So let's negotiate," I urged.

"Let's go some place and eat something first," she answered. "We need to get to know each other at least a little bit better."

"We can eat here," I said.

"Honey, this is Starbuck's. The stuff they got to eat here won't do nothing but piss me off. We need to go to Harold's for some chicken."

We decided to take one car, so she drove. We went to the Harold's over on 87th and the Dan Ryan Expressway.

"You want something?" she asked climbing out of the car. She drove a big SUV. She needed it. She was a big woman.

"I'll take a fish sandwich if they got one."

"They got one," she said.

I waited in the car while she went inside to order.

While Brit was gone, I pondered my relationship with Jiqin, the Chinese woman I was shacked up with over on Lakeshore Drive. Even *she* had initiated our affair. For her, it was initially a business arrangement. We ended up falling in love. At least I did. But I realized that I always end up with women that take the lead in forming relationships with me. I suddenly felt inadequate. Why was I always so at-a-loss around women?

When Brit got back, she climbed into the driver's seat, and sat for a moment pondering.

"You seem to know this city well," I commented.

"That's 'cause I live here."

"I thought you lived in Madison."

"No," she answered. "I was in Madison for the same reason you were there, to cover the rally."

I felt giddy as a teenager, and hated that I felt that way. I wanted to pursue this, whatever it was, and at the same time, I wanted to already know what to do. I watched her as she tore open the bag the food was in, and pass me my sandwich. She pulled a chicken sandwich from the bag, and bit into it.

"What are you getting me into?" I asked. It was like I couldn't stop myself from being the pupil when it came to women.

"We call it the life style," she said around a mouthful of chicken and bread.

"Sounds pretty generic."

"Don't let that fool you. This shit is kinky." She took another bite of her food.

I couldn't open my sandwich. I was too preoccupied with the possibilities before me. I was beginning to resign myself to my role.

"So how far can I go with you?"

"How far do you want to go?"

I wanted to say sex, but I couldn't even imagine that was on the table. But then I thought about it. If she got pissed and left or whatever, I'd lost nothing except an afternoon with a stranger. I took a deep breath and said it. I said, "Sex."

I had wanted to say something worldly like, "Your place or mine." But the single word 'sex' was all I could muster.

"Okay," she said matter-of-factly. "You want to fuck me." She swallowed and took another bite. "Is that all?"

The question caught me off guard. What else was there?

Then, as if reading my mind, she asked, "Do you want me to suck your dick?"

She rearranged her sandwich, tucking a piece of chicken back between the slices of bread. She didn't even look at me. Just as well, because I'm sure my mouth was agape with wonder. Even the worldly me wouldn't have come up with that, not at this early stage in our relationship.

She stuffed the last of the chicken into her mouth and began to chew vigorously. That's when she looked over at me. Not at me exactly. She looked at my unopened sandwich.

"You gon' eat that?"

"Huh?" I responded.

"I'll take that as a no." She took my sandwich from my limp hand, opened it, and bit into the catfish fillet.

"Yes," I answered.

"I'm sorry," she said. She immediately stopped chewing. "I thought you didn't want it."

"I don't want *that*. I want you to . . ., you know." All pretense of worldliness was completely gone.

I wasn't sure she had heard the last part of what I said. She immediately began tying into my sandwich again.

She glanced over at me, and did a little double-take.

"Crawl into the back seat," she said, "and pull you pants down. I'll be back there as soon as I finish this."

Naturally, I did as she said. Like an idiot, I literally crawled over the back of the seat I was sitting in. I could feel her looking at me as my right foot got wedged between the seat back and the wall of the car.

As I sat struggling to free myself, she opened the driver's door and climbed out. She closed that door and opened the rear door and climbed in.

"You are funny," she said, stifling a laugh and reaching over to help me free my foot. "You're like a child. How am I ever going to teach you how to be a dom?"

We pulled my foot free. I then unfastened my pants and pulled them down around my ankles, and off onto the floor of the car. I felt self-conscious. I looked around to see if anyone was near where we were parked.

"What's a dom?" I asked.

She didn't answer me. She knelt down on the floor, hanging my discarded pants across the back of the front seat I had just crawled over. She was more careful with my pants than I wanted her to be. I wanted her to hurry up and get started. Finally, she pushed my legs open, and stuffed my dick into her mouth. It wasn't hard, but she didn't seem to mind. She moaned, and took a deep breath through her nose. The car reeked of chicken and fish and pubic sweat.

As my dick got hard, she began to bob her head up and down on it. Her tongue was like magic working around the head. I came quickly, too quickly. But again, she didn't seem to care. She swallowed me down, and kept me in her mouth. Her tongue kept working the head. I was euphoric. I recalled a saying my grandmother used to quote whenever unexpected good fortune came her way: Look what the good Lord sent, and I ain't even prayed a prayer.

Brit, still sucking, began rubbing my stomach. I felt so pampered that Shorty began to rise up again. I expected her to begin bobbing again, but she didn't. She placed her fingertips just above my pubic hairline, and pressed hard on my bladder. The urge to pee shook me from my euphoria. I tried to scoot away, but Brit was a big woman, 250 pounds at least, and she was strong. She held me in place. I reached down to remove her hand, but it was too late. I could feel the urine leaking down, and I began to contemplate the mess I was about to make. But I was mistaken. There would be no mess. Brit sucked water from me like she was sucking soda from a straw. After three long pulls and swallows, she raised up and belched. The smell from her mouth was a strange mixture of chicken and fish and piss. There was the hint of ketchup and tarter sauce. I didn't know whether I liked it or not. She relaxed a little, and looked away. I didn't know if she was ashamed or merely nonchalant. Then she asked, "Do you still want to fuck me?"

"Hell, yeah, I still want to fuck you," I answered, "take your shit off."

Brit looked at me with a Mona Lisa-like smile. She knew that I wouldn't be able to turn down that pussy. She lunged her fat ass from side to side working her pants and drawers off. She reclined the back of the seat as far as it would go, then leaned back, spread her legs, and spread her pussy with her finger tips. She must have come as she was sucking my dick, because the smell of her pussy was strong, and added to the already pungent atmosphere.

I crawled between her legs, and began pushing her fleshy mid-section aside in order to enter her. She put her hand in front of her pussy.

"Hit me first," she said.

"What?"

"Hit me. In the face."

I could still smell my piss on her breath as she looked up at me, her unflinching eyes brown in the light through the tinted windows of her truck.

"But I don't want to do that," I protested.

"I want you to," she said. "That makes it better for me."

I felt uneasy about hitting her. My training was to hurt people when I hit them, and I certainly didn't want to injure her. I raised my hand, then smacked her lightly on the cheek.

She looked at me from one eye to the other as if assessing me. Then she hauled off and smacked me so hard upside my head that my ears rang and I began to see stars. I flinched when I saw her begin her swing, but my hands were occupied holding her ass and holding my dick. So, I couldn't block her punch.

Now I was pissed. I let go her ass, and grabbed a hank of her hair. I turned my wrist so that her face was pulled up and fully exposed. Then I let go my dick, and slapped her so hard I thought her nose might begin to bleed. I almost hit her with my fist. But at the last moment, I realized that I wasn't in any danger. I opened my hand and delivered three strikes to her face. With each blow, she gasped and hunched up her shoulders, but she made no move to protect herself.

My adrenaline was rushing. I leaned back and pulled her flat onto the seat. Then I pushed the fat of her stomach out of the way and slid straight into her. I braced my foot against the wall of the car, and pushed as hard as I could.

I wanted to punish her. Every time I began to feel the urge to come rise up, I willed it away. I wasn't done with her, yet. I wanted to push my dick through the back of her pussy. And as I pushed, she angled her pelvis up so that I was going in deeper and deeper.

I don't know how long we fucked. But when I finally slowed down and stopped, she was sweating and so was I. I was about to roll off her, but she stopped me. She cupped my head in her hands. She pulled my face to hers. She kissed me in the mouth. I thought about her drinking my piss, and hesitated. I could smell it on her. Along with the fish and the chicken and the tartar sauce and the ketchup and the bread and the funk of her pussy and our sweat, I smelled my piss on her breath. It reminded me of bacon frying for breakfast. Then the notion struck me, fuck it. I opened my mouth to let her soft tongue in, and I sucked it and swallowed, and offered her my tongue in return.

IV

"'Order Out of Chaos' is the motto of the ignorant feigning wisdom."

I had to give it to him. Menachem was supremely confident in his assertions. For him, it was clear as crystal what all of this meant. Not so for me. I wasn't sure what 'Order Out of Chaos' even was.

I hadn't meant to be so transparent, but before I could stop myself, I blurted out, "What does that even mean anyway?"

"It means that mankind is wandering aimlessly from a pathetic past to an equally pathetic future," he answered. "Nobody has a single clue as to where their own lives are going, let alone that of the lives of humanity as a whole."

"And the Masons claim to know?" I asked.

"Yes." His lip curled as he squeezed the words between clinched teeth. "They actually think they do, because they actually think they are controlling it."

"Well," I said, "they must be controlling something. Otherwise, we wouldn't be here plotting against it."

"They don't know shit," he spat. "They don't know a fucking thing."

It was this wrestling between knowing and not

knowing that brought to mind my last conversation with Ida, my second wife back in the day. That conversation concerned the notion of knowable verses unknowable. She eventually got me to see that not only was the universe much more complex than we mere humans could ever imagine, but it was much more complex than any organism, no matter how highly advanced, could ever imagine.

It was a tough sell, but once I understood the concepts, I kept turning them over and over in my mind.

Consciousness was the key. In all of creation, there are levels of consciousness, from the ameba and below to man and above. Each level of consciousness had its own realm of knowability. And just as Lucy knew nothing about how to make fire, Homo Erectus, who *did* know how to make fire, knew nothing about how to forge metals. We know how to forge metals and more, and the realm of what we can know seems limitless. But it isn't. We are as ignorant about the limits of the universe as Lucy was about making fire or Homo Erectus was about making steel.

What we as a species fail to realize is that advances in technology merely increase the range of things we don't know. Before telescopes, we had no idea about the far reaches of the universe. Now, with huge telescopes in space, we still have no idea about the far reaches of the universe.

"So what is the plan?" I asked Menachem.

"We first need to understand what they think they know," he answered. "We need to understand what they think they know that they think the rest of us don't know."

"So what do they think we don't know?"

"They think that we don't know that they are reeking havoc on the world," Menachem answered.

"But we don't know that," I offered.

"Maybe *you* don't know that, but I do."

It was Ida who got me to see that our ability to know is, in part, a function of our ability to perceive. Our ability to perceive is limited by our physical makeup, and our ability to extend that makeup. We see, hear, smell, feel and taste within a very narrow range. We have instruments that can extend that range, telescopes, microscopes, microphones and sensors of all kinds. But we are fundamentally limited to those five senses. Therefore, we define the universe in those terms.

Ida continued that there are aspects of the universe that transcend those senses. There are particles that we cannot see, hear, smell, feel or taste, even with our instrumental extensions. There are things about the universe that are beyond our ability to perceive, and are, therefore, beyond our ability to know. And because we imagine in terms of our perceptions, there are things about the universe that are beyond our ability to imagine. We cannot even imagine that which we cannot know.

"You say you know," I challenged. "But it sounds to me like you're merely guessing."

"Yeah," he came back, "but it's *educated* guessing."

"Educated guessing is still just guessing," I said.

Menachem smirked.

Even in the realm of what we *can* know, we cannot know everything. Heisenberg's uncertainly principle cites one example. One cannot simultaneously know the position and momentum of particles in quantum mechanics. In astronomy, we don't– and maybe cannot– know the size of the universe. And although we can detect the presence of dark matter, we cannot perceive it. We cannot see, hear, taste, smell or feel it even though it comprises a vast amount of the mass of the universe.

Part of our inability to know that which is in our own realm inheres in the fact that our tools of examination are inadequate. One cannot see, even with glasses, that which is unseeable.

In truth, we will never be able to do more than infer the presence of dark matter. That is the wonder of the universe. We cannot know it all.

It doesn't follow, however, that it cannot be known. It simply cannot be known by us.

"That's true enough," Menachem finally acknowledged. "Educated guessing *is* still just guessing. However, bear this in mind. Not all knowledge is provable knowledge."

"For example?"

"For example, will the sun rise tomorrow?"

"Of course it will."

"Can you prove it?"

"Certainly not."

"There you go," he said.

Ida's words were clearer now than ever. There is a realm of knowability in dark matter that we cannot know. The reason is because there is a whole different set of objects composed of the particles that we cannot perceive, objects from atoms to galaxies. And there is life there, life that is searching for the truth the way we are searching for the truth. They have their own realm of knowability, and that realm of knowability cannot know what we know. For creatures in that realm of knowability, our realm is unknowable because we are composed of particles they cannot perceive. They wouldn't be able to perceive us any more than we can perceive them. And the number of realms of knowability within the region of dark matter is infinite.

"What do you mean, there you go? There's no there-you-go there."

"Sure there is," he smiled. "You just haven't figured it out yet."

Some realms of knowability overlap. Creatures in these realms can share knowledge, can see, hear, smell, feel or taste the same things. Others are completely and totally distinct. Nothing that is knowable in one of these realms is or can be known in another of these realms. Such is the nature of knowledge.

"You sound like an idiot. There's nothing there to figure out."

"You'll see," he said, still smirking, "you'll see."

According to Ida, within the realm of human knowability, not everything is known by everybody. And those of us who have certain types and bits of knowledge go to great lengths to retain that knowledge for themselves. A case in point is the fact that there is a well-planned and well-rehearsed plan in place to enslave mankind. The specifics of the plan, however, are not clear. But they don't need to be. In fact, they cannot be. If the specifics were clear, the plan would become obvious, and an integral part of the plan is that it remain secret. Without secrecy, the plan would fail. That's why those of us who don't know the plan, and against whom the plan is directed, must act as if the plan were real even in the absence of proof, and, in fact, in the presence of proof to the contrary.

The only obvious manifestation of the plan is the system of laws that have been put into place by the planners for the benefit of the planners. The more I thought about it, the more I realized Reverend Milton was right. The planners purport the laws to be universal, applicable to everyone. But in practice they are not. They exist to control the masses, those whom the planners intend to enslave. As a result, these laws are a fucking joke. All of them. They are not and never will be applied for the benefit of the masses. They are and always will be manipulated in such a way that those who wrote the laws have a material advantage over those who are expected to obey them. Therefore, all members of the ninety-nine percent have an ethical duty to resist obeying the laws imposed upon them by the one percent, even if they think their actions will have no effect.

The reason is because everything in creation is conscious within its realm, and realms of consciousness do not necessarily overlap. They can overlap, but they do not necessarily overlap. The actions in one realm, however, can affect what happens in other realms even if those realm don't overlap. Viruses are not conscious of our realm of consciousness, and we are not conscious of theirs. But their actions in their realm can affect actions in ours. If someone gets a cold because of the actions of a virus, everything in our realm can change. But the virus will never know that. All it knows is what happens in its realm. In the same way, our actions can affect actions in realms above us, but we can never know how or to what extent. Such is the nature of the universe.

Ida and I had crossed that always-obey-the-law line many years ago. And I have crossed it many times since. But not without a price. We must always be prepared to pay the price of our actions. That price could end up being prison or even death. Ida has paid with her mental health. I have paid with my loneliness. I have no children, no family. I spend most of my time alone.

"This brings us back to the notion of architecture," Menachem said. "Architecture and numbers."

"So, let's hear it," I prompted.

He paused for a moment, his gaze flitting between two empty and equally uninteresting spots on the floor. Then he looked at me.

"Did you know that there is a pyramid with the all-seeing eye on top of the Israeli Supreme Court building here in Jerusalem?"

I didn't, but I didn't see the point he was making.

"So what?" I asked.

"It's the same pyramid and all-seeing eye that is on your one dollar bill and the reverse side of the Great Seal of the United States of America."

"Okay," I said, still uncertain of the point he was making.

Then he suddenly became exasperated by the fact that I wasn't connecting the dots.

"Damn it, man!" He said, "think about it. What the fuck have pyramids got to do with America anyway? There's no pyramids there! There's no pyramids in American history or culture. So why is there a fucking pyramid on the most circulated currency on the planet?"

He had a point, and I *didn't* have an answer.

But he was right. The all-seeing eye was a symbol that I and everyone in America had taken for granted, had accepted without question as a given in American life. But it wasn't. Pyramids had nothing to do with us. Hence, his question. What was it doing there?

It is said that in the final days, the dead will rise up and ascend to heaven. Sounds creepy, but there's no accounting for what people are prepared to believe. And actually, that's part of our problem as a species. Too many of us are too willing to accept as fact opinions offered to us by others. Those of us who can see this characteristic can– and often do– exploit it. Pyramids on the money was a case in point.

Somewhere along the line of time, someone suggested that we ought to obey orders given to us by persons who declared themselves better than us. The fact that some– and maybe even most– of us accepted this social arrangement without question appeared to suggest that all of us had acquiesced in it. Nothing, however, could be further from the truth. For some of us, *nothing* is better than us. And any attempt to alter that notion is met with stiff resistance.

"When was Israeli Supreme Court built?" I asked.

"1992."

"When was the pyramid put on the dollar?"

"1934," he said. "It went into print in 1935. But it was designed in 1776, the year the Illuminati was formed."

There are two kinds of slaves in the world. There is the slave that must be kept under lock and key. This person isn't really a slave at all. Given the first opportunity to escape, he'll do it. That's why he's under lock and key in the first place.

The second kind of slave will keep himself under lock and key based on what he's been told. This is the best kind of slave. This slave won't run away at all, because his thoughts are his lock and key. His own thoughts keep him in check. He is his own overseer.

Many thought paradigms can be used to keep a slave in check. Fear works, as does love and hope and, a perennial favorite, patriotism. The best of these, however, is religion. Get a slave to believe a religion, and he will be a slave until his dying day. Better yet, combine religion with love or hope or patriotism, and generations will be enslaved. It's the human condition.

It was Ida who pointed this out to me. She had said that *I* pointed this fact out to *her* very early on in our relationship, but I didn't remember that. It sounded like something I could have said, but so do lots of things. And over the years, I've said a lot of shit, shit that I now thought only a fool would have said. Maybe that was it. Maybe I was a fool.

I looked over at Menachem who was still staring at me.

Now his point was clear. Somebody in 1776 had the idea of controlling the world, creating 'Order Out of Chaos.' And 200 years later, the plan was still in place.

I didn't mention this to him, but it was obvious that their plan included exterminating Black people along with the elimination of Islam. It was clear that Order Out of Chaos meant a white only world, a world run and populated by white people.

These clowns clearly had to be stopped.

"So where are we going with all of this?" I asked.

"We're answering the what-are-you-looking-for question."

"And the answer is?"

"You're looking for me."

He was certainly right about one thing: I *was* looking for someone close to Benjamin. But I had not expected the conversation with that someone to go exactly like this one was going.

"Here's the part you don't know," he continued. "*I've* been looking for *you.*"

He looked me straight in the eye. I looked away for fear of revealing too much. But his gaze remained steady.

"You're a professional," he said, "but you were too easy to isolate. Israel has cameras everywhere, and your image popped up too many times at all the wrong times to be a mere coincidence."

He paused waiting for me to fill in some of the blanks.

I pondered whether or not I should reveal anything.

"I'll admit," he said at last, "that we couldn't find anything on you."

"We who?" I asked.

"The people I work with," he answered.

"If you know why I'm here, why are we having this conversation?"

"We *don't* know why you're here, but we're hoping it's for something we want, too."

I still wasn't prepared to reveal myself.

"Who *are* you with?" he asked. "You're not CIA or FBI or military. I'm ex-Mossad, and I still have contacts who can check stuff out for me. They found nothing."

I decided to venture a tiny bit.

"I work alone," I said. I relaxed waiting for him to make an attack. I was ready for anything he might try.

But he didn't make a move. I suspected he did not believe me, because nobody in this business works alone.

"So who's your target?" he asked.

"You already know the answer to that. The real question is, is *my* target *your* target?"

"It might be," he answered.

"Okay, try this one. Is my target a Mason?"

"Yes," he answered, "big time. He was inducted while

a student in the States."

"And what did they tell him?"

"Fuck if I know," Menachem answered. "I'm not a Mason."

"Well, when did you decide to make him a target?" I asked. "And how do I fit in?"

"You fit in, because you are here to do what you are here to do."

"How do you know I can do it?"

"We've been watching your reconnoiter routine. You know what you're doing. From that, we deduced that you've been trained in the black arts."

"How do you know you can trust me?"

"We're working on that part now."

"How do I know I can trust you?"

"We're working on that part now, too."

This was becoming complicated. There was no way under the sun that I could trust this man. But I couldn't let him know that. In fact, I was now forced to go along with him, because if I didn't, he would simply have me deported. At this point, I knew too much for him to allow me to stay. Worse yet, he might have me wacked.

"But you don't know for certain that I am who you think I am," I asserted. "Or that I can do what you think

I can do."

"That is correct," he answered back. "That is a part of what I am here now to determine."

"Then we have a problem," I said.

"How so?"

"You've been in this business for a minute or two. So you know that we're trained to never reveal who we are."

Naturally, I was lying. Never having been trained by any government, I didn't know what spies were trained to reveal or not. I was grasping at straws.

He pondered for a moment, then said, "One of us is going to have to reveal something to the other."

"And you know it cannot be me," I answered. "Especially if I am on an op."

He pondered for another moment. "Okay," he said at last, "my target is Nathan Benjamin."

I allowed myself one tiny reaction. I raised my eyebrows as I moved my gaze to the suitcase I had been packing just before Menachem knocked on the front door.

"The prime minister is a big target," I said.

"The prime minister must die," he retorted. "I'm just hoping you're the person we can count on to get the job done."

V

I hated to have to admit it, but Brit and I had started spending more time together because I liked the way she sucked my dick. Initially, she was reluctant to have me that close to her.

"Sex won't sustain a long-term relationship," she had said.

"I know that." I said it, but deep down, I didn't want to believe it. Deep down, I wanted her sucking my dick until she died, or until I died, which ever came first.

"So why do you want to just be with me?" she demanded. "Isn't fucking me from time to time enough?"

"You're a nice woman." I figured I couldn't go wrong with that one.

"You don't even know me," she said.

"Are you *not* a nice woman?"

"Maybe and maybe not. The point is, you don't really know one way or the other."

I hated being caught out like that. Yeah, she was right. I didn't know her.

"You just like me drinking piss from your dick."

Bingo! But I didn't say that out loud.

"But what about you?" she continued.

"What about me?"

"What about you reciprocating?"

"You want me to . . .?"

I couldn't even finish the question. She saw my dilemma, and laid it straight out for me.

"I want to squirt in your mouth," she said, "and I want you to drink it."

"Like mother's milk," I said.

"Yes," she said, as if I had asked a question. "You drinking from me would make me feel like I'm nourishing you, like a baby sucking from a tit."

"Only I'd be sucking from your pussy," I said.

"Yes, you'd be sucking from my pussy."

For someone who claimed to be a submissive, her tone and gaze were surprisingly direct. I didn't call her on it, though. I was still back at squirt. And again, she read me like a book.

"Some women squirt, you know?"

I was looking for the right answer, but all I could come up with was a question.

"Didn't you squirt in the truck that first time?"

"No," she said. "I almost did, but it stopped short." She continued, "If I had squirted, you would have known it."

What was it with this woman? I wasn't a complete rookie with women, but she always found a way to make me feel like one.

It had been only a week since we fucked in the back of her truck for the first time. We had sex a couple of times after that, but nothing kinky. Just plain vanilla wham-bam-thank-you-ma'am. The prospect of doing something more this time caused my pulse to quicken.

This was the first time I had been at her house. All of our other sessions had been in the back of her truck. I think she wanted to be sure she could trust me. This was also when I first met her young daughter.

I owned up and said, "I need to see you do it."

"Okay," she said, "but first, we need to resolve where we're going with this."

Maybe it was time for me to stop kidding myself.

"I like the way you drink from my dick," I said.

"And?" she asked.

"And what?" I asked back.

"And what about you reciprocating?"

I knew I was going to give it a try, but hell if I was going to give her the satisfaction of hearing it in words.

"Maybe I will, and maybe I won't," I said. "It's going to depend on the mood I'm in at the moment."

"We need to start now," she said.

"Get on your knees," I said. "I'll think about it while you're sucking my dick. And your fat ass better be thirsty."

She lumbered to her knees, and performed better this time than she did the first time. Then she looked up at me with those deep brown eyes.

I pretended to be doing her a favor, but in truth, I was eager to see her squirt, and to see how it tasted.

"How do we do this?" I asked.

"Work my g-spot," she answered, "hard."

"Okay," I said, "let's do it."

She led me into her bedroom and undressed. When she saw me still clothed, she asked, "Aren't you going to get ready?"

"Now yet," I answered. Then I told her to lie down, and pull her knees up to her chest and spread them.

"Yes, sir," she said. She was easing herself into a submissive mind set, getting into character.

I knelt down beside her and began to fondle her pussy. She closed her eyes, licked her lips, and began to lapse into the moment. She was wet at first, but before long, she began to dry out. I could feel my fingers begin to drag as I stroked her.

All at once, she snapped out of submissive mode, and hopped up to fetch a pump bottle of some kind of white, creamy fluid.

"Spread this on it," she said. She resumed her

position, and slipped back into a submissive state of mind.

I didn't know what this shit was, but it was good! I rubbed the top of her pussy hard, and she seemed to immediately relax. Her legs seemed tight initially, pulled up the way they were. But as I began stroking her, she began to allow her legs to loosen and spread more naturally apart.

That's when I slowly slid my fingers into her. Damn, she felt good! I played it down, but my dick was getting hard as a bat. I worked my fingers in and out of her for several minutes, and the more I worked them, the further into her I was able to get. And the further into her I was able to get, the more turned-on I became. It's almost as if the stuff we were using invited me to go deeper and deeper as her pussy opened wider and wider. I began to wonder how far into her I could push my hand.

All at once, I worried that I might be hurting her. But she appeared to be lifting her butt to take it in more. The harder I pushed, the more she lifted herself up. That's when I suddenly wanted to push it all the way in. I wanted to assure myself that she was okay, so I looked away from her pussy and into her face. She sensed my diverted attention, and returned my gaze.

"Don't look at me," I told her. "I don't want to see your pain as I do this."

I knew I was going to do it, and I knew it was going to hurt her. In truth, I *did* want to see her pain. But I was ashamed of the feeling. I hadn't come to grips with it the way I had come to grips with being a killer.

"Yes, master," she said. She closed her eyes and turned her face to the wall. Then she began to murmur, "Take me, master. Take me, master. Take me, master."

She grabbed my arm as she murmured, but I stopped her.

"Don't touch me," I commanded. "Raise your arms over your head and keep them there."

She did as I told her and kept murmuring, "Take me, master. Take me, master."

My breathing grew deeper and more rapid. I pinned one of her legs to the bed with one of my legs, and put the weight of my chest on her other leg at the thigh.

Her murmuring became clearly audible now, as she realized what I was about to do.

"Take me, master," she said. "Take me, take me, take me."

By now, I had the base of all four fingers inside her pussy with my thumb still working the outside button at the top. Now, the moment of truth. I slipped my thumb down to the opening, and forced my hand into her. My heart raced.

From the corner of my eye, I could see her pulling the hair on her head to avoid reaching down to stop me. Her murmuring was now a constant and sustained moan. This was wonderful. This fat-assed woman was helpless under me, or so it seemed.

My hand was inside her in a matter of moments. The big knuckle of my thumb cleared that hard opening, and my fingers curled automatically as they slid up along the back of her pussy. But it was too fast. I had wanted it to hurt. And maybe it did, a little. But I wanted it to hurt more. The fit was snug, but I could still move my fist around inside her. That's when the idea hit me to squeeze my fist as tight as I could, and pull it out. I knew it would be too big to get out, but the pressure inside her would be painful to her. So I did it. I kept my fist tight, rocked it from side to side, and pulled out as hard as I could.

She squealed. She squealed and grabbed my arm with both hands, her nails digging into my flesh. I didn't know a fat girl could arch her back as far as she arched hers. As I pulled my too-big fist against the inside opening of her pussy, I moved that same thumb knuckle back and forth across her g-spot. The effect was magic.

She began to tremble uncontrollably. Within moments, a clear puddle of fluid began to stream around my wrist. I angled my arm down just a fraction, exposing the hole from which the fluid escaped. It looked like a little water fountain in the park.

Still maintaining the pressure inside her, I shifted down until I could rub my nose and lips in her pubic hair, back and forth, back and forth. Her hair was rough against my skin. I wondered if she had cut it, and was now allowing it to grow back. The musk of her hair and her pussy and her ass was euphoric. But I waited too long. The fountain was off, the wetness soaking into the sheet under her ass. I wondered if she had some kind of liner to protect the mattress.

Then she surprised me. She lifted her hips up so hard, I had to struggle to maintain the pressure inside her where I wanted it. So I rolled my fist around in a circle, and yanked my fist although I knew it wouldn't come out. I could feel my knuckles rubbing across the boney nodules on the inside surface. I could feel the walls of her pussy squeezing in on my closed hand, and the lips of her pussy closing around my wrist. I could sense what was about to happen. I cupped my mouth over the top of her pussy right where it met my wrist, and it happened. It was warm like tea, and brackish. It didn't taste at all like pussy smells. But it didn't matter. It was warm and comforting and nourishing, and I drank like a baby on a nipple.

The next day, I moved some of my clothes into her apartment.

VI

"Twice under a space, . . ."

"Daddy, that's not the way it goes. It's 'Once upon a time.'"

Kelly wasn't really my daughter. She was Brit's daughter. But she liked calling me daddy, because she didn't know who her real daddy was. I liked it, too, so I let her do it.

"No, baby, this is a different story," I said.

"But it can't be *that* different."

"Sure, it can. It goes like this. Twice under a space, nearby and recently, . . ."

"No, daddy. It's 'Long ago and far away.'"

"This story isn't like those stories. This story just happened."

"Daddy, stories don't just happen. They happen a long time ago."

"Just wait, you'll see. Twice under a space, nearby and recently, it went to future that a little girl was lying in the bed listening to a story being told by her father."

"Is this story about me?"

She liked it when I played the father-daughter game with her. And the truth was, I encouraged it.

"No, baby," I said. "What makes you think that?"

"It sounds like me," she answered.

"No, baby, it's not you. Okay, here we go. Twice under a space, nearby and recently, it went to future that a little girl was lying in the bed listening to a story being told by her father. She asked her father, 'Is this story about me?'"

"It *is* about me," she cut me off.

"No, baby, this is a story about a different little girl all together. It's not about you."

"Well, why does it *sound* like it's about me?"

"I don't know. I guess sometimes little girls sound the same."

"But I just asked you if this story was about me," she declared.

"And I answered you," I said. I knew it wasn't nice to toy with little children, but I could not resist.

"I know," she said, "but the little girl in the story asked her father the same thing."

"She did?!" I questioned.

"Yes, she did. And that's why I wondered if it was about me."

"Well, it's not about you, honey. Just wait, you'll see. Okay, here we go again." I modulated my voice to affect innocence. "Twice under a space, nearby and recently, it went to future that a little girl was lying in the bed listening to a story being told by her father. She asked her father, 'Is this story about me?' And her father answered, 'No, baby, what makes you think that?'"

"Daddy, you're trying to trick me! This story *is* about me!"

"No, baby, it's not." I struggled to resist laughing. "This story is about a different little girl."

"Well, why does it sound like me?"

"Does it sound like you?" I asked.

"Yes, it sounds *just* like me. I said those same words."

"But we all say the same words, honey. We all say the same words over and over again. For example, how many times have I called you honey?"

"That's different."

"How so? Aren't you my honey?"

"Yes."

"Were you my honey yesterday when I called you honey?"

"Yes."

"Well, it's the same thing. I used the same words both times."

"Just finish the story, daddy."

"Okay. Twice under a space, nearby and recently, it went to future that a little girl was lying in the bed listening to a story being told by her father. She asked her father, 'Is this story about me?' And her father answered, 'No, baby, what makes you think that?' And the little girl answered, 'Because it sounds like me.' And the father said, 'No, baby, it's not about you. This is a different story about a different little girl.'"

I lowered my voice a little and paused in my story. Kelly was asleep. I kissed her on the forehead, and slipped from her room. I pulled the door closed behind me. I turned the knob so the sound of the latch clicking wouldn't wake her up.

I knew that the spot in the floor just outside her bedroom door squeaked when you stepped on it, so I tipped around it. I chuckled at my own sense of over-cautiousness. That squeak would hardly wake anybody up, let alone Kelly. That child could sleep through anything.

I tiptoed to the kitchen, and poured myself a glass of buttermilk. I sipped the salty coolness as I closed the refrigerator door, and began to contemplate the notion of a couple of chocolate chip cookies.

Just then, Brit ambled in and sat at the kitchen table. She pulled herself up as close to the table as she could get.

"Is that little bitch asleep, yet?"

"Please, don't call the baby a little bitch."

I knew she was playing a game, so I played along. We had played similar scenes before.

"Well, that's what she is."

"She's a little girl."

"She's a little attention-hogging bitch. That's what she is."

"Why are you jealous of a child, *your* child?"

"I ain't jealous. You fucking me, not her. At least, you bet' not be. 'Cause then I'd have to kill her. Or you."

"Don't be silly," I said to her. "You're not going to kill your own child."

"Then I guess it'll have to be you," she snorted. When it came to getting into character, Brit was a master.

Warming to the game, I pretended that she was getting on my last nerve. "If you touch me or her," I told her, "you will be in big trouble."

"Whatchu gon' do if I *do* touch her? You lucky I don't kick yo' punk ass right now."

Brit was a big woman, 250 pounds at least. She had dark, silky skin like dark chocolate. Her hair was straightened and black. It looked like Mexican or Native American hair. And she had a way of throwing her bangs from in front of her face with a snap of her head, especially when she was mad or trying to make a point.

"Listen, baby," I said, "let's change the subject." Now

I was getting into character.

"Why," she snorted. The corners of her mouth pulled down into a wicked-looking smile. Her lips parted slightly revealing coffee-stained teeth. "I like talking 'bout yo' ass."

"What did I ever see in you?" my character asked rhetorically.

"You stay with me 'cause you can't get nobody else. Won't no other woman put up with your whinny bullshit. The real question is why *I* stay."

"You stay because I pay your bills."

She paused for a moment as if contemplating the notion afresh for real. "Well, there is that," she said. She looked me up and down with her deep brown eyes. Looking at her expression, at her wrinkled up nose and furrowed brow, one would think she was considering whether or not to keep a pair of shoes with which she had just stepped into a pile of steaming dog shit. It might be easier to throw them away than to try to clean them.

"And in return for me paying your bills, you let me fuck you from time to time."

"And Lord knows *that's* a waste of time," she said.

"Meaning what?" I asked.

I pretended that my feelings were beginning to be

hurt.

"Wham-bam thank you, ma'am, twice a week," she said. "It's hardly worth me taking my draw's off."

"It's drawers, not draw's. And if they weren't so big, maybe you'd have energy enough to get involved when we did it."

"Now, I *am* gon' kick yo' ass!"

She pushed back from the table and hefted herself off the kitchen chair. She marched around the table towards me as if she were going to do something. She shifted her weight from one side to the other with each step, her legs wide apart.

As she approached me, Brit picked up the riding crop I kept on the counter behind the small television that was plugged in under the kitchen cabinets where we kept the cereal and flour and sugar. She was almost in striking range.

She reared back and swung at me as hard as she could, but she knew she was not going to hit me. I parried the blow, then slapped her hard in the face. She stopped to savor the pain. I snatched the riding crop from her hand, and slammed it on the table.

"Get on you knees," I ordered.

She hesitated.

"I said, get on your fucking knees."

"Yes, sir," she answered.

She shifted her weight back and forth as she worked her way down onto her knees. She used the table to help her keep her balance.

"You know what to do," I said to her.

She reached down with crossed arms to grasp the bottom of the tent dress she was wearing. It was pink gingham. She pulled the hem up over her head, then balled the dress up and squeezed it between her legs. She was naked, and I could smell how wet she was.

"Open you mouth and close you eyes," I said to her.

She did it. I unbuckled my pants, and unzipped the fly. I made as much noise and fuss as I could getting undressed. I could see the nipples of her tits getting firm. They were wrinkled and pushed out like giant raisins. I stepped in front of her and grabbed a fistful of her hair. Her breathing quickened. I angled her head back and slapped her in the face again. Then I stuffed my dick into her mouth. She let out a throaty groan as she sucked on me, and before long, she shivered and came. I squeezed harder on that wad of hair I was holding, and smacked her three times with my open palm on her upper back. She shivered again, and moaned around my dick. I could tell that she was squirting. I pissed in her mouth, and she drank it. I loved doing that! It felt almost like having an orgasm.

"Lie down on your left side," I commanded after the squirting stopped.

She did as I told her. Now I was standing over her.

"Lift you right leg up and spread your pussy so I can fuck you."

Again, she did as she was told. She spread herself by reaching around and pulling at the side of her pussy. The lips parted, and she was red on the inside. I reached for the riding crop, and smacked her with it right on her pussy. I hit her hard enough to be painful, but not hard enough to injure her. I hit her about ten times, paused, then hit her in the same spot ten times again. Only this time, I hit her a little bit harder. I lost count of the sets of ten I hit her. Five, six, ten. The hand holding her pussy open began to relax as she lapsed into subspace. The leg she was holding up began to lower itself. Its weight coming down caused Brit to turn onto her stomach. She was lying prostrate on the kitchen floor with her legs gapped open in a puddle of her own fluid.

I began beating her with the riding crop on her upper back, one shoulder blade, then the other. I varied the intensity and changed the angle of my strikes as I worked her upper back from side to side to side.

Then I started in on her butt. I began hitting her as hard as I could on one cheek, then on the other. The crop was leaving a mark each time I struck. Brit lifted herself slightly onto her knees so she could push her butt into each blow to make the pain more intense. Just as she began to push as hard as she could into each strike, I stopped hitting her. Now I was fucking with her head. This was like the Chinese water torture. She pushed herself all the way up onto her knees, her body begging for more, but I withheld the pain. I paused for several seconds to allow the anguish she was experiencing to increase.

At that point, she let out a little squeak, a little whine. This big-ass woman letting out that tiny winy noise almost made me laugh. She wanted so badly for me to hit her again, that she was on the brink of begging. But she knew not to beg, because then she would never get it. She was so conflicted, she was literally writhing in agony. So I took pity on her. I grabbed the lips of her pussy like I had earlier grabbed a wad of her hair, and squeezed them as hard as I could, digging my fingernails deep into her flesh. She almost never used a safe word, but I could see that she was about to, so I released my grip, and I pushed my hand into her wet pussy. I didn't ease it in. I pushed it in hard to make it hurt. She braced herself, rolled back onto her side and widened her knees to take it all in. I could tell her pain was intense, and my dick got hard as a brick.

Then, just as I pushed the knuckle at the base of my thumb by that bony ridge of her pelvis and watched the lips of her pussy slide slowly around my wrist, I felt a fresh supply of water running out of her. With my free hand, I used her dress to mop up some of the mess she had made on the floor.

That dress was going to have to go straight into the wash.

I pulled my hand out of her pussy, and straddled her leg, the one that was resting on the floor. I forced my dick into her rectum. I fucked her in her ass until I came.

VII

The obvious question, of course, was why did Menachem think Benjamin had to die? I moved it around in my mind a little, waiting for him to volunteer an answer. But he was off into something else. I knew Benjamin was the Antichrist. But did Menachem know that as well?

He was rambling on about something or other having to do with his experiences in the Mossad, something about, 'For by deception you can wage your war.' But I stopped him.

"Why do you want him dead," I asked.

"For the same reason you do."

"I want him dead because he is the Antichrist."

Menachem paused. "Is that it?" he asked.

Now *I* paused. "Is there more?"

"You don't know what he's done?" he asked back.

"I am trying to stop him before he destroys the planet."

"You're too late," he said. "He hasn't destroyed the planet, but he has destroyed democracy in the western world."

I was confused. Apparently, I had missed something. "I'm not sure I understand what you mean," I said.

"Okay," he answered. "I'm putting all my cards on the

table."

"Please do."

"It started with the bombing of the towers in New York."

"You know something about that?" I asked.

"Know something? I was there. I personally planted scores of the charges that brought down building seven."

"In the World Trade Center?!"

"Yes."

"You?!"

"Yes."

"It wasn't Al Qaeda?"

"Don't be silly," he said. "There's no way Al Qaeda could have pulled that mission off. That's a given."

"What the fuck are you talking about?"

"I'm talking about the World Trade Center complex."

"I heard what you said. I'm just not sure what you mean."

"Okay," he said. "*You* tell *me* how tower seven collapsed."

"I don't know how it fell," I said.

"But you do know that nothing hit it, right?"

"I do know that, yes."

"You do know that airplanes hit towers one and two, but nothing hit tower seven, right?"

"Right."

"But at the same time, you don't believe that someone planted explosives in that tower to demolish it."

"I didn't say that."

"Oh, I see," he said. "You believe someone planted the explosives, but you don't believe it was me."

"I don't know what I believe." And I didn't.

"The Mossad trains its officers in the use of thermite explosives, and I and my team planted scores of thermite explosives in tower seven several weeks before September 11th. Other teams planted similar charges in towers one and two. I know what I am talking about, because I was there. Israel's Mossad destroyed the World Trade Center complex."

I was stunned. I had heard the rumors. I had even seen some of the films. But here it was coming right out of the horse's mouth.

"But why?" I asked. "Why would Israel want to do something like that?"

"Now, that is the $64,000 question, isn't it? Why indeed?"

"And the answer is?"

"Look around," Menachem answered. "What do you see?"

"Not much," I answered. And I wasn't lying.

"Well, think about this. An operation of that magnitude took months of planning," he said. "We had to get the architectural designs of all three buildings, study them, and determine where best to place the charges. We had to determine how much thermite would be needed. Then we had to buy the stuff. Nobody just has that much thermite just sitting around. We had to determine where we would be when we detonated the charges. We wanted to be able to see the buildings go down. That takes planning, months of planning. Years of planning. And do I need to tell you who supplied us with the materials a job like that requires? We didn't pack it on a boat and float it over. Somebody already here got it for us. And why was there never a forensic investigation done at the site? Why was the steel with thermite residue whisked away and made into a ship? There is thermite residue in the soil. Why is nobody looking at it? Because they built a park there?!" He chortled and paused feigning waiting for an answer, then he continued, "We all had day jobs like ordinary people. We were movers for Urban Moving. That was our cover for months. And after the charges in the towers were planted, a few of us stayed behind to video tape our work, to watch the buildings fall. The cops caught us, but a couple of phone calls to the right people got us out."

"And you think Benjamin was behind it," I said.

"I think the Masons were behind it. Benjamin was just the front man."

"Okay," I said. "What about the $64,000 question?"

"Yes," Menachem mused. "You don't see much because you aren't meant to see much. This has all been done in secret."

"By who?!"

"The Masons!" He said it again, "the Masons."

I tried to think of all the people I had known over the years who had been Masons. Not many people came to mind. And those who did weren't people I actually knew. They were acquaintances at best. In short, I didn't know any Masons.

"That's the point," he continued, "that I was trying to make about the Israeli Supreme Court Building. It is a Masonic structure. The Masons planned Tel Aviv the same way they planned Washington, D.C. The same forces that were at work then are at work now, planning, scheming."

"But planning and scheming what?"

"World domination," he answered. "They want to take over the world."

"But they can't do that," I protested. "How do you

take over the world?"

"Don't you understand? They're already doing it. They've taken over Israel. And because of the September 11th event, they've taken over the United States of America."

"What?! You're mad!"

"The United States Congress is already irrelevant," he continued. "You now have in your country a revolving monarchy. The president runs the whole show. He is a king with absolute power and authority. He kills people anywhere in the world on a whim! And nobody holds him accountable. Nobody *can* hold him accountable, because he has absolute power."

There was a lump in my throat. I wanted to refute what he was arguing, but I didn't have any facts immediately to hand.

"Since nine-one-one," he continued, "the United States of America has been in a heightened state of readiness bordering on martial law. Under the guise of protecting the country from terrorist attacks, President Bush issued an order that gave him the right to put into place directives that did not need to go to the congress first. Every president since Bush has reissued that same order year after year after year. It is pursuant to that order that the National Security Agency now has the authority to monitor everything Americans do. It is pursuant to that order that unmanned killer drones now fly in U.S. skies. It is pursuant to that order that terrorists-- even Americans-- may be killed anywhere in the world for whatever reason the president warrants with no trial and no recourse."

I knew this country had serious problems with regard to Black folks, but I had no idea that its imperial reach was so far.

"Where are you getting this information?" I asked.

"What? You don't believe me?"

"Oh, yes," I answered, "I believe you. I just find it hard to believe that so much of this madness goes unnoticed by the press."

"You don't understand. The mainstream press is part of the problem," he said. "It's the same here in Israel. The same people who run the news outlets here run the news outlets in your country."

"And the Masons are behind it," I said.

"The Masons are behind it," he confirmed.

I thought about it for a moment, then asked, "So, why are we killing only Benjamin?"

He looked at me as if the notion had never crossed his mind to broaden the scope of the plan.

"Benjamin, after all, is only the front man. You said

so yourself. If we kill him, the Masons will only put someone else in his place."

"But we don't know who the Masons are," he said.

"That is correct," I countered. "But we *do* know who benefits from their actions."

"Namely?"

"People with money," I answered, "lots of money."

"So we should start killing rich people?"

"Not merely rich people," I clarified, "super rich people. People worth a billion or more."

"And finding them would be easy," Menachem mused.

"Right," I answered. "They list themselves in *Fortune* magazine. Just compile a list from *that* list, and start shooting."

Menachem thought for a moment. Then he said, "You're right. The richest families in the world need to be killed. All of them, every man, woman and child, on sight, no questions asked. It is these families that control the banks, that control the politicians, that control the governments of the world. It is they who have stolen our democracy."

"If we ever had it," I said as I nodded in agreement. Then, slowly, as if it were the moon rising over Lake Michigan, the notion came to me that the two groups we were contemplating were one and the same. Billionaires *were* Masons. Milton was right. America *is* the great Satan. But not *just* America. All of western culture is the great Satan. And it is billionaires that have made it so.

"We could let Benjamin go," he said.

"No!" I was adamant. "Benjamin gets to die anyway."

"Because?" he asked.

"Because Benjamin is the Antichrist."

VIII

I couldn't believe how much I had come to enjoy beating Brit. I had always thought of myself as a considerate person with regard to women. I had always thought that men who beat women weren't real men, that they were cowards who picked on people who were weaker than themselves. But smacking Brit in the face gave me such a rush! And I felt no guilt, because I knew that she wanted me to do it. She said so. In plain English.

I was discovering an aspect of my character that I had no clue existed. It brought to mind the day Jiqin told me about her plan to remodel the building we lived in back then. She had Chinese workers– illegal immigrants– do all the work. She confided that she kept them in line by telling them that I might kill them. At the time, I found the prospect exciting. I hated to think of myself as someone who enjoyed killing people, but, in fact, I was exactly that. I was a person who enjoyed killing people. And once I decided to look the notion straight in the eye, I was able to come to grips with it. I was a killer, a natural born killer. And I loved it. I loved the power that I had to cause a man to die, to watch his eyes focus on nothing and stop moving. It gave me a rush that felt as good as an erection.

Hitting Brit gave me a similar rush, gave me a similar sense of power. In the case of killing a man, it was the rush of watching him die, knowing that the flow of time and history has been permanently altered because of my hand. In the case of hitting Brit, it was the sense of power in watching her writhe, listening to the sound of the blow, then hearing her react, hearing the distress in her voice, hearing the timbre change as I increased the pain. That sense of power made my dick grow harder, and I loved it.

I began to wonder how it always happened that I met women who thought I was someone other than who I really was. That's when it struck me. Maybe they were the ones who saw the real me. Maybe it was I who was blind as to who I really was. I had often heard that one of the hardest things for a person to know is what it is that he wants. The reason, of course, is that it is so hard to know who he is. Who he is determines what he wants. And if he doesn't know who he is, how can he know what he wants? He may think he wants what he says he wants, but be at a loss to determine why, after obtaining it, he feels such a profound sense of dissatisfaction, why what he wanted isn't what he wanted after all.

Looking back over my life, I had always wanted, or thought I wanted, a woman who was my equal, someone I could talk to, someone who loved what I loved, someone who was going in the same direction in life that I was going. But it never seemed to work out. All the women in my life were gone, the latest, of course, being Jiqin, the Chinese woman who found me the day I got shot and took me to her uncle who nursed be back to health. Jiqin, her uncle and her crew lived with me for months before burning the house we shared to the ground, then disappearing without a trace.

Now here I was with a woman I scarcely knew feeling a sense of satisfaction I hadn't felt . . . ever. Had I been fooling myself all this time? Had I been pretending to want a woman who was intellectual and artistic and creative and all those things I had thought I wanted in a woman? Or more to the point, had I been hiding from the real me? Had I been unwilling to face the man who I really was? Or was the sadist who loved killing people merely discovering another facet of himself, a facet that loved inflicting pain on women.

That's when I began to wonder how it would feel to beat her and fuck her, then kill her, watch the color drain from her face as I slipped a knife under her rib cage and into her heart while I still had my dick in her throbbing pussy. My reaction to that mere thought was so intense that I had to catch my breath. I shook my head to clear that thought away, it was so disturbing.

IX

Menachem raving on about the Masons again caused me to remember something Reverend Milton and I had talked about years earlier. Once more, Milton was doing most of the talking.

"Nixon is the one who fucked everything up," he had said.

Milton never did figure out the connection, but maybe Menachem had the pieces Milton was missing.

"It was Nixon who said that Blacks were the problem, and that something had to be done about them without them knowing about it," Milton told me.

I wasn't sure I believed him, so my reaction was muted. I simply said, "Uh-huh."

He went on to say that Nixon appointed four Supreme Court justices, Burger, Blackmun, Powell and Rehnquist. I recalled him extending his fist for emphasis, then raising a finger for each of the justices Nixon appointed. He raised them slowly as he carefully enunciated each name. Burger. Blackmun. Powell. Rehnquist.

Thinking back on Milton's musings, could Nixon have been a Mason? What about the four justices he appointed?

Milton was as passionate about the topic of Nixon then as Menachem was about the Masons now. He narrowed the treachery down to one Supreme Court decision that changed everything. That decision was Imbler v. Pachtman.

"That one case changed everything for Black people," Milton said. "After that one case, Black men began going to prison in record numbers. And it was Nixon's appointees who decided it."

I didn't have much to say at the time. I mean, how does the student react when the teacher is holding forth?

"Nixon's appointees solved what Nixon saw as the problem with the country. We were the problem, and after Imbler, all of us were going to prison, were on probation, or were on parol," Milton said. "It took years before we saw the connection," he continued. "Richard Pryor saw it first. He visited prisons and saw that it was just us in there."

I did vaguely recall having seen one of Richard Pryor's routines where he mentioned visiting a prison and seeing only Black men there.

I didn't understand it at the time, but Milton had proof that the Imbler decision was bullshit. He researched it while he himself was in prison.

"It's all in the footnotes and earlier decisions," he told me, "because the Imbler court didn't expect anybody to read the footnotes or really old cases."

Apparently, he was right. For years, nobody had noticed that the earlier case the Imbler decision indirectly rested on didn't say what the Imbler court said it said. That case was Thibodaux v. Town of Thibodeaux, an 1894 case out of New Orleans. That case didn't give prosecutors absolute immunity as the Imbler court said it did; it gave them qualified immunity. But in typical white-boy fashion, the Imbler court decided on the outcome it wanted, then concocted the rational that would support that outcome. It was bullshit from the very beginning. Nixon wanted a way to control Black folks without us knowing about it, and the Imbler court gave it to him.

"That was in 1976," Milton told me. He continued, "The Imbler decision undid everything the Ku Klux Klan Act in 1871 was meant to do. The Klan Act was specifically passed to protect Black people from the outrageous acts being perpetrated against them by prosecutors in the post-civil war south. But after Imbler, prosecutors were free again to do whatever they wanted to do, and they began sending Black men to prison in record numbers, because prosecutors could no longer be sued in civil court for malicious prosecutions."

Milton had paused for a long moment allowing me to ponder the weight of what he had just said. I admitted it was slowly sinking it.

"Ten years after Imbler was decided," Milton resumed, "Reagan signed The Anti-Drug Abuse Act of 1986, and ordered Ollie North and the CIA to flood the Black community with crack, a drug the CIA knew from its operatives in South America to be super addictive. From that point on, cops arrested us, and prosecutors sent us to prison. The Imbler decision, Reagan's war on drugs, and the plague of crack were the white man's dream come true."

That was the end of Milton's lesson for that day. But

listening to Menachem now, and given that the incidence of crime has not abated since the Imbler decision, the question that arose in my mind was, What was the problem that Nixon saw that Black people posed?

The answer that gradually seeped into my mind as Menachem expounded on about the Masons was that we posed a threat to the Masons' plan for world domination, the New World Order. I recalled that throughout the history of this country, Black people have stood in opposition to the tyranny of the government, not out of high-mindedness, but because we bore the brunt of this countries tyrannical actions. Little by little, I began to realize that all of our heros were soldiers in the struggle of the day, from the American revolution to the civil rights movement. All of our heros stood in staunch opposition to the inhumane policies of the United States government. We are practiced in organizing, rallying and speaking out against the kinds of policies the Masons would need to put into place in order to achieve their goals. More than that, it is Black people who started the revolution in the 60s and 70s, Huey Newton, Stokely Carmichael, Bobby Seale. As a people, we have demonstrated that we can mobilize to bring this country to its knees. *That* is why we were a problem.

The part that Milton never figured out was the Mason

connection. Nixon was probably a Mason, and all the Nixon appointees were probably Masons as well. It is the Masons who are responsible of the misery of Black people in America. I didn't learn this until much later, but historically, it was the royal family of England that profited most from the European slave trade. Over fifty members of the British royal family and aristocracy founded the Royal African Company in 1663. Chief among them were James, Duke of York, and King Charles II. The royal family profited from the sale of Black people for nearly a century and a half. All the men in the royal family were Masons. And it was the Masons who were putting Black people in prison today to be used as free labor. The Masons profited from the enslavement of Black people once, and they are taking steps to do it again. Milton was just one step away from putting the whole puzzle together.

Then, as if on cue, Menachem said, "If we want to save the world, billionaires must die. All of them, be they royalty from Europe or the Middle East, executives of corporations or banks, or investors from the U.S., China or Russia. If they or their families are worth a billion dollars or more, they must die. Maximilien Robespierre had the right fucking idea." Menachem paused for a long moment. "I did a paper on him in school. I had forgotten how powerful a writer he was." He paused again, then said, "'We seek an order of things in which commerce is the source of public wealth rather than solely the monstrous opulence of a few families.'"

"Was that you or Robespierre?" I asked.

"That was Robespierre from a speech he delivered in February of 1794."

"The brother had the hook-up," I said. I don't know how I remembered that Robespierre was the father of the French revolution, but I did.

Menachem chuckled. "It was from a speech on the political philosophy of terror. Six months later, he was dead. The man was a megalomaniac."

"Are you seeing some kind of pattern here?" I asked him.

"Well," he said, "we are treading a path he tread two hundred years ago, and at the end of which he died. One can't help but wonder."

"Not everyone who deals in terror dies," I said.

"True enough. Just consider my namesake."

"So, stop worrying."

"I'm not worrying. I'm merely musing."

"So, stop musing. We've got work to do."

Then, as if consumed by a fit of melancholia,

Menachem lit into his own story.

"It must be the human condition to have to make decisions with not enough facts," he said. "'The secret of freedom lies in educating people, whereas the secret of tyranny is in keeping them ignorant.' That's another Robespierre quote. And governments use the secret of tyranny against their people all the time."

"Right on," I said.

"My grandmother came to Israel years ago as an idealist," he continued. "Her name was Carol, and she was a New York beatnik. She had read Kerouac and Kierkegaard and fancied herself knowledgeable. She had been to Woodstock. She had heard Jimi Hendrix play the Star Spangled Banner. She knew what was what, or so she believed."

I waved my hand in a little circle as a gesture for him to cut to the chase. It didn't work. He was warming to his topic.

"She wanted to help create a better world, so she came here to work on a kibbutz. The kibbutz was supposed to be a utopian community."

He paused to gather his thoughts, or maybe to settle deeper into the mood. His glance wandered to the ceiling as he remembered the details of his grandmother's story.

"She would be dreamy-eyed as she talked about it.

Her voice would express a sense of wonder."

As did his as he remembered her.

"She was already pregnant with my mother when she got here. She referred to it as a free-love gift from some guy at the concert. Carol was a true libertine. She was full of life and hope."

Then his glance returned to me.

"She never learned about the history of this country. She never learned about *Irgun* and Menachem Begin and the massacre of Palestinian men, women and children in 1948. Or if she did learn, she somehow managed to fit it into her notion of peace and love. People often do that.

"When my mother was born, Carol stayed in this country, became a citizen. She is the one who talked my mother into joining the Israeli military as a young woman. She is the one who talked my mother into naming me Menachem. The point is, for all of her philosophical readings, she was an ignorant woman, and this government kept her that way in order to use her services for its own benefit."

"Maybe she kept *herself* that way," I offered. He didn't hear me.

"Eventually, my mother *did* join the army here. She eventually learned that the *Irgun* was integrated into the IDF after the British left, and became ashamed of being a soldier. Carol, however, was unpersuaded. When my mother was killed in some training exercise, Carol took the medals the government gave her, and displayed them for years in our living room. And now here I am hoping to use *Irgun* techniques to undo everything Carol believed in and hoped for."

I didn't know quite how to react. I settled on, "Life is a bitch."

But Menachem's musings set me wondering again. Back in the day, Menachem Begin was a thug, a murderer, a common hooligan. Today, he is a hero.

Then it struck me. The United States of America is the single most militarily powerful nation in the history of mankind. Only one tactic can defeat her: terror. Terror tactics work, and she knows it. Israel is Israel today because of terror. South Africa is free because of terror. France is France today because of terror. Viet Nam won the war against America with terror. Afghanistan won the war against the Soviet Union with terror. America is more afraid of terror than any other single tactic on the planet, because it works. She is using terror tactics of her own in order to maintain her position of power in the world. The problem for America is that states can't use terror without becoming the target of terror, and states present a much bigger target for terror than a terrorist does. America's target is small; the target she presents is huge. America is doomed, and terror will be the agent of her demise.

X

"Twice under a space, nearby and recently, it went to future that there was a little girl who lived in a kingdom in the shadow of a mountain. The little girl was a princess and her father was the king of the realm.

"One day, the king got sick, and the princess was very worried. She was worried because the king's illness didn't seem like a normal illness. The princess believed that the king had been placed under a spell.

"So the princess wandered out into the realm in search of a way to break the spell. She searched far and wide, but found nothing that she could use to help her father."

I paused in the telling of my story.

"So what happened," Kelly asked.

"The king died," I answered.

"What do you mean, he died? You can't end a story like that."

"Well, why not?" I asked. "People do die."

"Good kings don't die. Not in bedtime stories. Change the ending," she said. She snuggled into her pillow and stuck her thumb back into her mouth.

"But wait," I protested. "Why can't a good king die?"

"Change the story." Kelly spoke as forcefully as she

could with her thumb still in her mouth.

"Oh, alright," I said. "So the princess came back to the castle after having traveled far and wide throughout the realm. And when she returned to her palace room, there were three women waiting for her."

"Do these women have powers?" Kelly asked.

"Oh, yes, they have great powers. Their powers are in their names."

"So, what were their names?"

"One was named Uchina Guchi."

"Is that like abracadabra?"

"Yes, but a lot more powerful. Uchina Guchi had the power of flight, and when she flew, magical things happened in the land below her, in that anything she thought came to pass. Flowers grew, butterflies fluttered, and birds chirped."

"Wow! I like her. Who were the other two?"

"The second one was Lakshmi Singh. She had the power to cast spells on people."

"Good spells?"

"Any kind of spell she wanted. She simply uttered her own name, Lakshmi Singh, and any spell she could think of would happen to the person she pointed at."

"Wow! That's better than Harry Potter. One spell does everything."

"Then there was Ofeibea Quist-Arcton."

"That one is long," Kelly said.

"Yes, but her power was very special."

"More powerful than the other two?"

"Not more powerful, just more special."

"How?" she asked.

"Ofeibea had the power to block and undo other people's spells."

"So she could undo Lakshmi Singh's spells?"

"Lakshmi Singh's spells were the only spells Ofeibea could not undo, because they were friends."

Kelly snatched her thumb from her mouth. "So she could cure the king!" Then she thought about it. "Unless Lakshmi Singh cast the spell."

"Exactly. She could cure the king. Because the king was not under a Lakshmi Singh spell. So the princess took Ofeibea to the king's room, and Ofeibea uttered her whole name, Ofeibea Quist-Arcton, and the king got instantly better. In a few days, he was completely well again.

"After he got better, he asked Uchina Guchi and Lakshmi Singh and Ofeibea Quist-Arcton if they would go around throughout the realm and grant his people their fondest wishes. And the three of them said they would. And the people were happy and loved their king, and the king reigned for many years. The end."

"That was a good story," Kelly said. "I like stories with happy endings."

Her voice trailed off and her thumb slipped out of her mouth.

I leaned down, and kissed her on her forehead. "Good night, baby," I said.

"Good night, daddy."

Such a simple sentiment, and yet so powerful. Good night, daddy. It reminded me of my childhood, but I always associated it with alcohol breath and my mother and grandmother yelping in pain. Good night, daddy.

That's how it would sometimes start. My father would come home late, and I would mummer, 'good night, daddy,' hoping that he would go straight to bed. More often than not, though, it wouldn't work. He would come in late on a Friday night and go to the bathroom. I would hear his water splashing into the water in the commode. Then he would come out and ask what's for dinner. It would be late, well past midnight, and mamma would answer that she would get something for him right away or there would be something in the oven already or maybe there would be nothing left for him to eat. It wouldn't matter. There would be no right answer. He would never be satisfied with whatever answer she gave, and that answer would always be the beginning of a beating for my mother and for Grandma Daughter.

In my little mind, I thought that was the way it had to be. At least at first. At first, it seemed like a script. Like a drama that got acted out every Friday night with minor variations. In fact, it *was* a script that he took glee in acting out. For him, men were supposed to beat their women. That's how their roles got defined. That's what made him a man. That and drinking lots of whiskey. He took pride in the amount of whiskey he could consume. He bragged, "I drinks a whole *lot* of whiskey."

Then one day, he began slowly losing his grip on his faculties. He became forgetful. Eventually, he died. I still remember the dreams I had around that time. Maybe because I had them to this day from time to time, dreams of him in pain and suffering.

They always seem to end with me kissing him as he lay in a coffin. Sometimes, I dreamed that *I* was in the coffin. My last coffin dream was like that. For whatever reason, I was being fitted for a new coffin. I lay down in one, but it was too short. I could feel the top of my head and the bottoms of my feet touching the ends of it. So I climbed out of it. As I was climbing out, I noticed that it was built in such a way that its length was adjustable. It had screws along the side panels that could be loosened to allow the side panels to slide against each other to make the coffin longer or shorter, and for the balance of the dream, I used screwdrivers and pliers and anything else I could find to help me loosen the screws. I woke up before I managed to loosen enough screws to lengthen the coffin. Maybe it was because I knew the coffin was really for Daddy.

Daddy had been a tall, muscular, light-skinned man with a big lumberjack's neck. People thought he was good-looking because he had curly hair that was almost auburn, and almond-colored eyes. With his small, turned-up nose and thin lips, he looked almost like a white man, lying there in that coffin. The dream would almost always end with me bidding him, 'good night, daddy.'

I pulled the covers up around Kelly's shoulders, and rubbed my hand across her head. Her hair was braided into four short pigtails, and smelled of sweat. I eased from her room, and latched the door behind me.

XI

Rachel, Rachel, I've been thinking
What a cruel world this would be
If the boys were all transported
Up and over the northern sea.

I was having a flashback to a time when I could move my consciousness from my body to another plane, a space somewhere outside my body. Back then, my body was like a robot that I could move in and out of at will. This was the first flashback I'd had in years since my tour of duty in Germany. It now had a different character. There were colors in my awareness, reds and yellows and greens and purples, iridescent like the highlights on an oyster shell, and the words were slithering from the colors like maggots from moldy cheese.

I remembered hearing this rhyme from the little girls in the neighborhood in Chicago where I lived when I was a shorty. At least, that was what I told myself. In fact, I was not sure where I'd heard it before. Maybe I was making it all up.

I felt like a character in a video game. Things looked real enough, but I knew they were not. At least, I thought I knew they were not. In a consciousness shift, it was hard to be sure what was real, and what was not. I was truly out of touch.

My character looked a lot like me the way I looked now. But he also looked like me the way I looked thirty-five years ago. He was old like me, but somehow, he still had the hair I had as a young man, short and black and kinky and rough to the touch. And it was full. Not the horseshoe around the back of my head like is was now. He was cut like the young me, thin-limbed and narrow across the shoulders, but he had a potbelly like the old me. I had the same russet brown skin, the same long face and shallow cheek bones, the same light brown eyes with the asynchronous blink. But the bags under my eyes were just as pronounced as they were today. My skin didn't seem to sag as much as in real life, but it still had that crepe thing happening.

In this game, the little girls from the old neighborhood were taunting me. They thought I was cute, but they could not come right out and say it. Nice girls didn't do things like that. So they sang this stupid song. It was a metaphor for their own true feelings. But being the literal child that I was, I always wondered who Rachel was. And where was the northern sea anyway? I had never heard of such a sea. And what was on the other side of it? Maybe the other side wasn't so bad. I spent so much time wondering about the nonessentials, that I missed the true meaning of the message.

But now I understood. I understood, but way too late. The little girls were gone. They were probably all dead by now.

The image of one of them began to coalesce amid the colors in my head. Her name was Mary Jane, and she was my sweetheart. At least I thought she was. Maybe I merely *wanted* her to be my sweetheart. She was a light-skinned little girl with freckles and kinky, blond hair. As much as anything, I was intrigued by the notion of a little black girl having light hair. She and a little friend she used to hang with– I didn't remember the friend's name, but they looked enough alike to be sisters or cousins or something– used to lure me into a secluded corner of the playground. Then they would look around and giggle and turn their backs to me and flash their panty-clad behinds before running off and laughing insanely. I never quite understood what was so funny. I did, however, enjoy their antics.

I also enjoyed watching them from a distance. We never talked, so the notion of saying something never crossed my mind. Besides, what would I say? There was nothing *to* say. We were children. But watching them was always fun. They played with dolls together, pushed blocks in the sandbox together, ate lunch together. The best part was when they looked at me and pretended to be whispering together. I loved it, and I hated it. I loved the attention and the little tingle I felt watching them look at me. I hated that I didn't know what the feeling was that I was having. I was not sure I knew now. But even not knowing what it was, I would rather have been with it than without it.

Another image began to coalesce in my mind. An image like a video began to gather itself together of me as a child standing with Mama on the corner of 63rd Street and South Park Boulevard in Chicago. In this video, Mama was big like she had gotten after Daddy died. She looked like she weighted 350 pounds. I was not sure she weighted that much in real life. She certainly didn't weight that much when I was the age in real life that I was in this vision.

Double decker buses used to turn off of west-bound 63rd Street onto north-bound South Park Boulevard at that corner. It was a tight turn, because the steel columns for the el that ran overhead above 63rd Street restricted the available turn space. Sometimes the rear tire of the bus would clip a portion of the curb as the bus pulled slowly around. Mama and I had been on this corner many times before, so I knew to keep a safe distance back.

This particular morning, I was standing my customary distance away. But a man in a grey flannel suit sauntered carelessly close to the side of the bus as it crept around the corner. He was close, but not too close. I could see the space between him and the bus.

All at once, the man collapsed onto the ground. A woman in a wide-brimmed, straw hat shouted, "The bus hit that man." She was wrong. The bus hadn't touched that man. In fact, when he first collapsed, I thought he might have been playing some kind of strange all-fall-down game. But the people waiting for the bus reacted to the woman's shout. They began to move around the fallen pedestrian in an agitated fashion. One man wearing workman's overalls leaned over the man on the ground and asked, "Are you okay?"

The woman in the wide-brimmed hat was now nowhere to be seen. The bus stopped short of completing the turn. The driver opened the doors and hopped out shouting, "I didn't hit him. I didn't hit him."

I looked up at Mama, and said, "The bus missed him, Mama. I saw it." The driver looked me in the eye, and I could see and feel his anguish. He desperately wanted the truth to be known. And I wanted to tell it. Back then, I thought that revealing the truth would make everything all right again. But I was a child. I knew the truth, but it was worthless. Mama quickly grabbed me up, and whisked me off down the street. As we sped away, I could hear the driver pleading with the man to get up. "Com' on, man," he said, "you gon' cause me to lose my job."

As Mama scurried me away, I craned my neck around to see what was happening on the corner. The man in the grey flannel suit remained motionless on the ground. Mama pulled my head back forward. "You didn't see nothing," she said. "You don't never want to get involved in stuff like that."

I wondered, stuff like what? Revealing the truth about what I saw? What could possibly be wrong with that? Was it wrong to tell the truth?

In truth, the truth was something I knew inside. It came to me spontaneously, and it came with no regard for space and time.

I remembered that I was a little boy again, about nine years old, about the same age I was that day on the corner. I was in my home standing in front of a mirror admiring a new sweater or shirt I was wearing. Or maybe I liked the fit of my pants or the feel of my gym shoes. There was something about what I was wearing that made me feel invincible. Standing there in front of that mirror, I suddenly had a vision of me running. I was being chased, and I was out running the people who were chasing me. The vision was so strong, I could feel my legs beginning to twitch. Then the vision vanished.

Later that same morning, my class went to gym. We usually stayed near the playground for gym, but this day, Mr. Wylie, a pimple-faced young man who was always clearing his throat, took us to the park about a block from the school. As soon as we stepped onto the plane of grass, I recognized it as the setting for the vision I had earlier.

Mr. Wylie pulled a football from the canvas bag he had brought with him. On the first play from scrimmage, I got the ball and ran for a touchdown. At least six boys chased me as I ran the length of the field. The truth revealed itself to me, then became manifest less than two hours later.

That day on the corner with the man in the grey flannel suit lying on the ground, I knew it was *not* wrong to tell the truth.

But now, as an old man, during this flashback, I wasn't so sure any more. I had lived a lie for so long and in so many different way, I simply didn't know. As a rule, I didn't care. But this day, wiggling deep in the back of my mind, I wondered. Maybe I didn't see what I thought I saw. Could the bus have hit that man, and I willfully refused to see it? Could that bus driver have wanted me to lie on his behalf? Maybe everything I remembered was wrong. The colors were swirling and swirling and swirling, the reds, the yellows, the greens, the purples.

All I had were childhood memories, memories of little light-haired girls pushing boxes in a pit of sand, or flashing their panty-clad bottoms, then running off and laughing insanely. Maybe all of that was simply wrong. Or maybe they were merely phantoms of the illusion I was having, apparitions of the oranges and blues swirling in a gossamer fog. Maybe everything I knew was shit.

Rachel, Rachel, I've been thinking
What a cruel world this would be
If the *girls* were all transported
Up and over the northern sea.

XII

"Ubonjee-e-e-e!"

Wow! I hadn't been called that in years. And certainly not by any one in this town. I turned around to see who this could be. I saw a man with fair skin and almost no hair on his chin coming out of the bank building I was walking in front of. I recognized him instantly. He had a quick, animated laugh. He hadn't changed much over the years. I was envious. He was shorter than I was by several inches, and he walked with his chest poked out in an effort to exaggerate his height. He also rolled up onto his toes as he walked, again trying to look taller than he was. But everything about him was short. His legs, his neck, his arms. His hands and fingers were short and thick.

"Aba ben Israel!" I called out to him.

"Man, I *thought* that was you. But I'm not used to seeing you with so little hair."

"It's been a minute," I said. I wanted to pop him in his mouth for that crack about my hair.

We hugged and dapped and grinned at each other and looked each other up and down. He wore a long, burgundy robe trimmed in gold, and a matching kufi.

"It *has* been a minute," he said. "What the hell are

you doing here in Tel Aviv?"

Ubonjee was the African name I had taken years–indeed, decades– ago, back when black was beautiful and it was always nation time. Aba was one of the brothers who claimed to be one of the true Israelites. Even back then, he was quick to point out that today's Israelis were not Jews at all, not the true Israelites. The true Israelites were Black people who roamed North Africa years ago. He had books written by rabbis that explained how the white people who call themselves Jews today stole our identity, and continue to palm themselves off as the real people.

"I'm here on business," I answered. "I'm a photographer looking to get some shots for a magazine I'm working with."

Aba was a professional drummer. He had played drums for thirty years that I knew about, five of which had been with Sun Ra's group. As of that chance meeting, I hadn't seen him in ten or eleven years, maybe longer. I knew Aba when I lived incognito in Chicago after the building over in South Shore burned down, after Jiqin disappeared, after Reverend Milton needed space from me in order to feel safe.

"When did you start taking pictures?" he asked. "When I knew your ass, you were down and out, sleeping over in Jackson Park."

"That was a tough time for me," I answered.

"I know," he answered back. "I'm the one who got you that first contract. Or had you forgotten that?"

I hadn't really been sleeping in the park back then. I had a car. So, naturally, I slept in that. This was shortly after Jiqin and her people had disappeared. Maybe a month. Had I run into Ida again at that point? No! I bumped into her and Aba at some kind of metaphysics meeting. It was at the library over on 73rd and Exchange. I went there to use the bathroom, and Ida was holding forth to Aba and a couple of other folks in one of the conference rooms. I listened in for a few minutes, and watched her gesticulating wildly to make some point or other. It wasn't until then that I realized that she hadn't been using any notes. This was Ida off the top of her head. I was impressed. She seemed so powerful, so in-control. Is that what being crazy does to people? She came over and hugged me. Then she stepped back.

"You stink," she said. "You need a shower."

I felt ashamed and embarrassed. I didn't want to have to admit it, but I did.

"I'm kind of down on my luck," I said. "My ship hasn't come in yet."

"What do you need?" she asked.

Just then, Aba walked up to us.

"You had it goin' on, baby," he told her. "You really brought the spirit down."

"Thanks, Aba," she said. Then she changed her tone, and said, "Aba, this is my friend . . ."

Before she could say my name, I blurted out, "Ubonjee. My name is Ubonjee."

Ida picked right up on it.

"Ubonjee is looking for a little something to occupy his time right around now, and I know you know a lot of people who need things done, and done right."

"I know some people," Aba confirmed. "What do you do?"

"I'll leave you two to talk," Ida cut in, then she slipped away. It was years before I saw her again.

"I do whatever needs to be done," I answered.

"Have you had any training? Do you know how to hurt people?"

"They're hurt if I hold back. If I don't hold back, the pain goes away."

"I might know some people," he said. "But you'd better be good. If you fuck up, they see to it that *your* pain goes away. Understood?"

"Understood," I answered.

My first hit was through the people that Aba knew. Small fry, really. Some white-boy drug dealer who thought he could scam a brother out of some smack. They offered me a couple of large, and I snapped like a salmon. They gave me the piece I needed to do the hit, and the dude's schedule of rounds. It was an easy job at bargain basement prices, but it got me into the business. I had steady work after that, mostly out of town, and for a lot more money.

"I started doing pictures between contracts," I said, "because some of my clients wanted proof that the job was done."

"And," Aba chimed in, "I guess it makes for a good cover."

He raised his eyebrows slightly, then relaxed them. That was his way of letting me know that he knew I was in Tel Aviv on a job.

"It makes a good cover," I confirmed.

"So, who's the mark?" he asked.

"I can't tell you that," I answered. "Besides, you don't really want to know."

"'Cause if you told me, you'd have to kill me?"

"Something like that. But it wouldn't be me doing it."

"Then who?"

"Don't ask so many questions, man. It would be the

client."

"So if the client does hits, why isn't the client doing *this* hit?" Aba was suddenly dead serious. His light and easy demeanor were gone. He knew something.

"This was no chance meeting, was it?" I asked.

"Yeah, it was," he answered. "And I'm the one taking the chance."

"Do we need to talk?"

I began to walk in the direction I had been walking before Aba stopped me.

"Don't move," he commanded. His expression was more one of caution than one of authority.

I stopped and relaxed, waiting for I didn't know what.

"We are standing in a blind spot right now. We can't leave it together. We want anyone who sees this tape to think you went into the bank, then came out again after I did."

"It's your move," I said. "How do we proceed from here?"

It dawned on me to ask how he was so sure this was a blind spot, but I decided not to.

"Remember this address and get there in exactly 2 hours," he said. "I'll have somebody pick you up for a meeting."

He gave me a number and street name, and abruptly

launched off across the street. I watched him for a good two minutes as he walked briskly in the other direction across the street, that burgundy robe with the gold trim flapping around his ankles.

Before bumping into Aba, I had been on my way to take a Gray Line bus tour. I had felt that I needed to act more like a tourist. Now, continuing that trek, any feeling I had of being a tourist was gone. Not only was I acutely aware of the fact that there were security cameras in Israel everywhere, but I was also preoccupied with trying to figure out how Aba knew that he could intercept me at that particular spot on my trek.

Naturally, I forgot about the bus tour. I needed to find out where this address was, and how best to get there. I didn't want to take a taxi, because I didn't want my destination logged. I didn't want to rent a car, because they sometimes have tracking devices. I needed to borrow a motor scooter. I called Ariella. I remembered that in one of our conversations, she mentioned that she drove one.

"I need your help," I told her. "I need some wheels."

"It'll cost you," she said.

"I can pay," I answered.

"Where are you? I'll come pick you up, and you can drop me off back at home before you run your errand."

I agreed, and told her where I was. Twenty minutes later, she pulled up to the curb next to me.

"Hop on," she said.

I did.

As we drove, I began to muse about that first hit that Aba had gotten for me. I tried to remember what he had said about the contacts he had back then. And through it all, I tried to find a connection between who he was then, and how he ended up in Tel Aviv now. I drew a blank. I looked around as I rode hoping to see something that might give me a clue as to why Aba ben Israel would be here. I noticed lots of signs in Hebrew and lots of men in wide-brim, black hats, but nothing that helped me make the connections I was trying to make.

That's when it came to me. How the fuck was I going to find this address. I didn't read Hebrew, and I had no idea how to find anything in this town. Aba must have known that I would have to ask someone for help getting there. What could he possibly have been thinking? I was clearly going to need a guide. One that I could trust.

"What do you know about Menachem?" I asked Ariella. I guess I was fishing for an answer that would give me a clue as to whether or not I could trust *her*.

"Not much," she answered. "I try to know my clients, but he doesn't reveal much. Why do you ask?"

"I need someone I can trust."

"You can trust *me*."

"You're too easily bought," I said.

"I'm not easily bought at all."

"But you can be bought," I confirmed.

"If it's business, I can be bought. It's what I do. But if it's trust, I will take a confidence to the grave."

I had no choice. I had to confide in her.

"I need to meet a friend," I told her, "but it has to be . . ." I searched for the right word.

". . . in confidence." She finished the sentence for me.

"Exactly," I said. "No one can know who I'm meeting or where. I also want to avoid the cameras if I can."

"Avoiding the cameras is going to be hard," she said, "depending on where the address is."

I gave her the address, and she proposed a plan. We would drive around town for an hour or so, sightseeing. We would make a couple of stops, buy a couple of items to be used in a disguise, an over-sized shirt, a wig. Then we would go to a restaurant near my target location for coffee. While at the restaurant, I would sneak out the back, don the wig and shirt, put a stone in my shoe to camouflage my characteristic walk, and hobble a couple of blocks to my rendezvous. She would tell me how to get there. After my meeting, I would come back to the restaurant's back door. Then we would leave together out the front, and bike back home. I agreed, and we sped off.

"What would you like to see?" she asked.

"What is there to see?" I asked back.

"The Caesarea Obelisk," she said. "It's a few clicks away, but it's an interesting site."

This must be the obelisk Menachem was telling me about. Odd that Ariella would suggest it as a place to visit. I didn't want to arouse any suspicion, so I agreed.

"Cool," I said, "let's go."

We took Rothschild Street to get to the Caesarea National Park. Once there, we parked the bike and approached it on foot. It was set in a field surrounded by stones that looked like they had been part of a different structure, probably parts of an older Hippodrome. There was a line of trees thirty or forty feet behind it. According to the plaque, it was made of red granite, and it did have a rosy color.

As I stood looking, Ariella ventured around to the other side. She was out of view for over a minute. Then she emerged looking down at something in her hand. She ambled back over to where I was standing.

"There was a man back there," she said. "He was passing out cards."

"This is hardly a heavily trafficked site, is it?" I asked, "Why would he be passing out cards here? There are a lot more tourists over by the water."

"He said he wanders around the entire Hippodrome site passing them out."

She gave the card to me. It read, *Das Innerste Feuer*.

"We've got to go," I said.

"What? Why? Where are you going? I want to see the rest of the park."

I remembered Lillian warning me many years ago. 'You are in grave danger,' she had said, 'we must leave here at once.' She further warned, 'No one must see your face.'

I lowered my head and turned back towards the bike. I stuffed the card into my pocket.

"We are leaving," I said, "and we are leaving right this minute."

XIII

Over the weeks that followed, Brit and I enjoyed intense play sessions together. I bound her, I beat her, I fucked her, all in varying combinations. In the back of my mind during many of these episodes, though, the image of me sliding a blade into her side kept nagging. My dick got harder at the very thought. Whenever the image presented itself, I would stuff my dick into her and thrust as hard as I could. I wanted to purge the image from my mind. I wanted to cleanse myself of the urge to kill someone who loved me, and whom I loved, or could love. I would plunge in and out of her frantically, but it never worked. The more worked up I got, the more I wanted to do it. In time, the image began to take on a life of its own. It became so vivid that I could almost feel her warm blood escaping the gash I had opened in her, her blood flowing over my fist as I twisted the blade to increase the flow. I could feel her blood gathering between our bodies, and I could feel myself wallowing in it, rubbing it all over my body, smelling it, tasting it salty on my mouth.

"I need to cut you," I finally told her late one night after thrusting in and out of her for what seemed like forever.

She got excited.

"Yes," she said, "I *love* edge play. I was wondering how to bring it up for us to try."

I rolled off of her. "Go get a knife," I told her.

"Yes, sir."

She hopped up and headed for the kitchen. I could hear her opening her utensil drawer and rummaging around for a blade. She returned with a paring knife.

"Take that back and get something big. Bring me the biggest knife you own."

She came back with a 12 inch, curved, skinning knife.

"We used to go fishing with this," she said.

"Perfect. Now go get some rope."

She was animated now. She couldn't wait to feel the surge of fear and the rush of adrenalin. She was anticipating having massive orgasms for an hour or two or three. She thought she would be in ecstasy forever. And she was right. She would be. She trusted me completely. Or rather, she had completely thrown caution to the wind.

"I don't have any rope," she said upon her return, "but I have this packing twine. Will that do?"

"It'll do just fine. Now lie down."

She climbed back onto the bed.

"Front or back?" she asked.

"Lie on your back, and spread your legs."

Slowly and methodically, I tied each of her four limbs to the corners of the bed. The twine was thin, so I wrapped it around her wrists and ankles multiple times to ensure that she could not break free. As I got the last of her limbs secured, I could feel the euphoria washing over me. I was about to do it. My dick was as hard as the wooden headboard of the bed. I began to get nervous. I forced my breathing to remain steady. I grabbed her panties off the floor, and wadded them into a ball.

"Open your mouth," I told her.

I stuffed the wadded panties into her mouth, and wrapped twine around her head at the mouth and wad to hold it in place. Now she couldn't scream. Now I could tell her.

I stood at the foot of the bed looking down at her brown body spread wide, a huge mound of flesh that would soon be wet beneath me. I could smell her sweat and her pussy. She was clearly excited.

"I am going to kill you," I told her.

She thought I was playing a role. She thought we were doing a scene.

"I'm going to kill you," I told her again.

I didn't move from my position at the foot of the bed,

and I stared directly into her eyes.

The wave of fear that washed over her was palpable. Her eyes grew wide and her body temperature began to rise. I could smell it. Her glance began to dart from side to side. She lunged her head up and down and from side to side. She yanked at her restraints, but they held her fast. I climbed onto the bed between her outstretched legs. I was on my knees sitting back on my heels.

"Have you ever heard of death by a thousand cuts?" I asked her. "It's an ancient Chinese torture technique."

She pulled so hard on her restraints that she farted.

"Did you just fart on me?"

She turned her head from side to side as fast as she could to communicate, no.

"But somebody farted," I told her. "If it wasn't you, who was it?"

She couldn't talk because of the gag in her mouth, so she grunted and moaned. She issued three short grunts for, "I don't know."

"You don't know?" I asked her. "Well, I think it was you." My voice was low and even and sinister.

I leaned down to one side from my kneeling position and retrieved the knife, her knife, from the floor. I placed it onto her copious abdomen.

"You have one chance to survive this," I told her. "I'm going to fuck you, and it had better be the best pussy I've ever had in my life. Do you understand?"

She frantically nodded, yes. I was lying and she knew it, but she nodded, yes, anyway.

"Present you pussy," I told her.

She did. She spread her knees as best she could, and angled her pelvis up so I could enter her. I slid into her, and rocked in her for what seemed like a long time. In truth, it was probably only about five minutes. In truth, I really didn't want to fuck her anyway. This was just the ritual. In truth, I wanted to kill her.

I pulled out of her, and sat back on my heels again. I took the knife, and poked the tip of it into both her nipples. I didn't break the skin. I just poked them so she could feel it.

"Does that feel good?"

She nodded, yes.

I ran the point of the blade several times up and down her stomach. I poked the blade tip into her clitoris.

"How about that?"

She nodded, yes, again.

Now the moment of truth.

"Say, 'goodnight, daddy,'" I told her.

She began to cry. Tears began running down both

sides of her face, and her nose began to run. She shook her head from side to side in protest. She pulled at her restraints. She tried to buck herself free.

"Say, 'goodnight, daddy,'" I told her again.

She resigned herself to her fate and closed her eyes. She grunted four times for, goodnight, daddy.

I straddled her abdomen like a horse for better leverage. She whimpered now, knowing the end was near.

I looked down at her face, and for the first time, I saw how much she resembled Kelly. They had the same broad face, the same broad nose and thick lips, the same crescent hairline. She grunted, goodnight, daddy, again, and I could hear Kelly. I could see Kelly with her thumb in her mouth, nodding off to sleep. I positioned the knife just under Brit's rib cage. This time the point broke the skin, but only just barely. All I had to do was push, and I'd feel her warm blood oozing out of her, just like the image I had seen in my mind for weeks. All I had to do was push. I drew back and thrust the blade down at her chest, then turned my hand over at the last second so that I hit her in the chest with the handle butt. I did that six, seven, eight times. Each time, her sense of terror increased. She was horrified.

Her breathing was labored in part because I was

sitting on top of her, and in part because she expected to die at any moment. Her heart was pounding. I could feel it with the sides of my thighs. I could see her pulse throbbing at the side of her neck in time with the pounding I was feeling in my legs.

Goodnight, daddy. The voice I was hearing was Kelly's. I tried to push Kelly's voice from my head, but I couldn't do it. I couldn't kill Brit. I couldn't kill Brit, because in killing her, I would be killing Kelly. And there was no way I could kill Kelly. She was a child. She was *my* child.

I dismounted, and got dressed as quickly as I could. I cut one of her hands free, then left. I left knowing I would never see her again. I left knowing I would never see Kelly again. I was glad I had not given up my apartment, that I had someplace to retreat. And for the first time in I couldn't remember how long, I cried.

But it wasn't the crying, *per se*, that I couldn't remember. It was this feeling of being a monster, something so loathsome, that I hated it. I hated it, and I hated myself. I hated me, because my mother hated me.

But it had not always been that way. She used to love me. When I was a shorty, three, four, five, she loved me. She used to hug me and kiss me and let me cuddle her.

She could walk into a room and I would run to her and hug her and bury my face in her stomach and smell her. And she smelled wonderful. I loved smelling my mother. Her neck, her hair, but I especially loved the smell of her when I buried my face in her stomach.

Before long, I realized that the smell I loved wasn't at her stomach. It was below her stomach, but not as far down as her thighs. I would smell that smell, and be in ecstasy. I smelled other parts of her body to see if they smelled like that particular part, but no other part did. Only there. Eventually, I would bury my face right at her crotch, and inhale.

One day, I asked her about it. She was standing there, and I had my face buried just below her stomach, and I inhaled as deeply as I could. I was drunk on my mother's aroma.

"What is that I smell, Mama?"

"I don't know, honey. What does it smell like?"

"I don't know, but it smells so good."

"Like what, honey? Where do you smell it?"

I took a small step back, and pointed to the spot where the smell came from, below her stomach, just at the tops of her thighs.

"There," I said. "What is there that smells so good?"

That is the moment that my life changed. That is the

moment when I became a monster. Mama stepped away from me three full paces. Her expression told me that I was a creature she had never seen before, and hoped to never see again. Her mouth literally hung open, her eyes widened, and she looked at me as if she had never seen the true me before. I approached her to hug her again, but she pushed me away. Somehow, I had revealed myself as the monster. Somehow, I was no longer loveable. I didn't deserve hugs and kisses and cuddles. Without realizing how it happened, I had become reprehensible.

It was confirmed later that day when I walked in on her talking on the telephone with someone. She looked at me with surprise in her eyes. I wasn't supposed to have caught her talking, and I could tell that she was wondering how much I had heard. She turned her back on me, and shielded the mouthpiece with her hand before hanging up the phone. I never knew what she was saying, but I knew she was discussing the creep she had just discovered.

I was crushed, but I hid it.

I wanted the warmth from my mother that I used to have, but from then on, all my affection from her was perfunctory. She would hug me, but not like before. Her kisses were short pecks on the cheek, not the bury-her-face-in-my-neck kisses that I used to get. Cuddles were now like handshakes. Maybe she thought I couldn't tell the difference. Maybe she didn't care, but I never felt her warmth again. Never. I wondered if it was the fault of whomever she had been talking to on the phone.

In time, I had to replace the desire for her warmth with coldness. I had to steel myself to being unlovable. In time, I became comfortable with the fact that I was a creature, a monster, a freak.

We each learned to play our respective roles in the mother-son dynamic. She played her role; I played mine. We played the roles so well that I eventually became comfortable in the role-playing. I pretended that her affected affection was genuine. And most of the time, it worked. Most of the time, I could forget that she wasn't the same as she used to be. I even began to react to her ministrations as if they were real. I even allowed myself to believe they were real. When I came home from Ruby's party that night after Ruby's mother had caught us having sex and smacked us both and threw me out of the house, Mama comforted me and told me stories about her youth and how she and Daddy were young and in love together. It felt almost as if she really cared. And in retrospect, maybe she did, a little, the way Belle cared for the beast or Ann Darrow cared for King Kong.

But deep down, I knew it was a sham. I knew she was holding back. I knew I was still the monster.

Thinking back on it, the reason I loved being babysat by Miss Blue was because Miss Blue's affection was real. I could almost see her now, a small woman, flat-chested with no curves to her body. She wore straight-cut house dresses in dark blues, greys and browns. She wore black comforts with short heels and shiny, black toe-caps. She didn't see me as a freak. And she always had cookies and milk ready for me when Mama brought me to her house.

Her friend, Miss Abbey, was the same way. She saw me for who I was. I think that's why she was able to show me who *she* was. I still remember how I felt the day she showed me what was under that patch of hair between her legs. I was fascinated. I wanted to touch it. I was transfixed. I couldn't take my eyes away. I could smell it. At the time, I had not remembered smelling anything like that before, and it affected me in a strange way. My breathing became deeper as I tried to pull more of the aroma into my nostrils.

I now know that what I was smelling on Miss Abbey was the same thing I had been smelling on Mama. I liked that smell. I liked it; I craved it. And Mama withheld it. Now Mama's love was gone forever. I couldn't blame her, though. After all, how do you love a freak?

In time, I wanted to hurt myself. If I hurt myself, I could show her that I was on her side, that I agreed with her. Then maybe she would see that there was something left in me to love. Then maybe she could bring herself to hug me the way she used to.

I started by hitting myself, on the arms, on the chest, in the face. But that didn't cause enough pain. In fact, it didn't hurt at all. That's when I began killing things. Small things at first, bugs, worms. Then bigger things. Mice when I could catch them. Then I discovered cats. Mice squeaked when you tortured them. But cats knew how to scream, and their screams were music to my ears. I inflicted in them the pain that I couldn't inflict in myself. And they were stronger than mice, so the music lasted longer.

The first cat I tortured by pouring turpentine in its ass. I was about ten. It howled and scooted around the yard dragging its ass in the grass. I did that to a few of them. Then I discovered that I could tie the tails of two cats together with a length of cord, then loop them over a low-hanging branch, one on one side, one on the other. They would each think that the other one was responsible for it being suspended by its tail, and claw the other one in order to get free. They would claw each other to death. I loved it! The screeches. The blood. The hardest part was getting rid of the bodies. I buried a few before I discovered the sewers. Lots of dead cats ended up in the sewers.

It was my experience dumping cats into sewers that led me, years later, to dump one of Jiqin's victims into a sewer. The victim's name had been Juan. He was one of the Mexican aliens she had been trafficking. He had run out of money, and had hoped to scare her into letting him live at our house rent-free for a month rather than for merely a week. He pulled a knife on her, and within fewer than ten seconds, he was on the floor fatally stabbed with his own blade. Her Uncle Yuen, a member of her crew I called Chico, and I dumped his body into a sewer that same night. But that was years later.

Eventually, I stopped killing cats. Killing them no longer satisfied me, so I stopped killing altogether– until Ida and I shot up that little police station on the west side. That's when the lust for blood was rekindled. And the way Ida looked at me that night, I thought she saw the truth, the truth of who I really was. And it was what she saw in me that scared her as much as seeing death up close. She, too, saw that I was a creature, a monster, a freak. Could I have been smiling as I was killing those men? Whatever it was, it scared her. Eventually, it drove her crazy.

XIV

Oddly enough, I was beginning to recall more of the sundry conversations Reverend Milton and I had over the time that I knew him. Not all of them were important. Some of them were downright frivolous. And I rarely remembered them. But this one popped back into my head apropos of nothing at all. Or maybe it was the fact that he was the one who put it on my mind that there was a centuries-old conspiracy in place to kill off Black people world-wide. He said it was the King Alfred Plan.

It wasn't really a conversation. Rather, it was him musing aloud. We were sitting by the lake looking out over Montrose Harbor. We were smoking a joint or two . . . or three. I was fixated on the bobbing of boats rocking on the waves, their masts swaying back and forth.

And out of the blue, Milton said, "Who the fuck do these honkies think they are, anyway?"

I had no answer. In fact, I thought the question was rhetorical. So I kept on swaying with the boats. It felt like the whole world was rocking, and I could feel myself beginning to panic wondering if I would fall off. After what seemed like five minutes, but what in reality was more like 25 minutes, he blurted out, "It was that fucking Nietzsche."

"What?" I asked.

"It was Nietzsche."

"What about Nietzsche?" I was still rocking with the boats and gripping the grass I was sitting in with both hands to keep myself from flying off into space.

"Man and superman," he answered. "Don't you remember?"

"Remember what?" Nietzsche didn't fit in with the boats, so I had trouble piecing this all together. Besides, I had more important things to worry about. The world was quaking, and I had to protect myself.

"Nietzsche came up with the notion of man and superman."

"And?" I asked.

"He was a racist bastard, that Neitzsche!"

Hearing it said that way was like an epiphany for me. "Wow," I said. Then I said it again, "Wow."

I was high as a motherfucker. And so apparently was Milton. I wanted him to shut up so I could get back to the boats and concentrate on keeping all of creation from sliding off the planet. But he was on a roll.

"Honkies think they superman," he said. "That's why niggers are so dangerous."

I said, "Wow," yet again.

"That's why Jesse Owens was so dangerous."

"Jesse who?"

"Owens," he answered. "Won four gold medals in Berlin in 1936. Hitler must have been pissed!"

By now, I had stopped listening to Milton. I could hear him without listening.

I almost teetered and fell over. It was only by a force of will that I was able to remain upright and still bound to the earth. I wanted to go for help. But I knew that if I stood up, I would be a goner. I had to maintain my grip on the clumps of grass I was holding. My head began to spin. I knew it was because the earth had begun rotating in the opposite direction. Damn! The sun was going to be rising in the west now. Boy, that was sure going to fuck shit up!

I wondered why Milton couldn't tell that the earth had changed its rotation. But then I saw why. He was still prattling on about Neitzsche or Hitler or somebody.

"White men think they are supermen because they are white. That's why they are afraid of us!" he said. "Every time a Black man outdoes a white man, it challenges the myth that white men are supermen."

Now *he* was having an epiphany. He stood up and began pacing in the grass. I wanted to warn him how dangerous standing up was given how the earth was in such tumult. I could see him swaying and bobbing with each step. He was weaving even when he didn't step, when he merely stood still. I closed my eyes, because I didn't want to see him fly off into space.

"They used to think we were mentally *and* physically inferior to them, and subservient by nature. But now they think we are just mentally inferior to them. And since mental prowess is superior to physical prowess in their minds, they can keep the myth alive."

That's when I saw it! That's when I saw the power of his words! He was using words to stay grounded to the earth. Talking was the key. If I kept talking, I would be able to stand up and go for help. I decided to recite the Gettysburg Address.

"Four score and seven years ago, . . ."

Milton kept on about men and supermen.

"That's why smart Black men are so dangerous."

". . . our fathers brought forth on this continent, a new nation, . . ."

"Smart Black men are a direct affront to the myth. If Black men could be supermen, white men would be nothing."

". . . conceived in Liberty, and dedicated to the proposition that all men are created equal."

Milton laughed aloud, then receited:

"Dumpy Honky sat on a wall,
Dumpy Honky had a great fall,
All the king's horses and all the king's men
Couldn't put Dumpy Honky back together again."

Milton literally rolled in the grass laughing at his version of that old nursery rhyme.

I couldn't remember any more of Lincoln's speech. But maybe that was enough. I tried to stand up. That's when the earth began to really shake. I fell face first back into the grass. I could hear the traffic on Lake Shore Drive roaring by. I could hear the crunch of dry grass under my face. Through the drone of 'white men's new nation' and 'black men created equal' looping in my head, I could hear Milton still musing.

"You okay, boy? Maybe you better just lay there for a while."

I tried to utter some words, but my mouth was stuck. I think I wanted to say, Black men's nation, but it couldn't come out. I'm not sure how long I was there, but when I became aware again, Milton was still at it.

"What are they going to do when niggers begin to play hockey and drive fast cars?"

Black men's nation? I decided it was hopeless. I decided to let go and allow myself to float away on the ether. I closed my eyes and felt the earth drift away beneath me.

When I woke up, the sun was sinking, and Milton was asleep in the grass beside me. He began to writhe, so I decided to wake him up. I grabbed his shoulder and shook him. He started awake.

"Oh, man," he said. "That was a fucked up high."

Thinking back, he was right. But now the ground was level again, and still. I stood up just to make sure I still could. My stance was a little woozy, but I was good. I was glad to be back down.

"What was in them joints?" I asked.

"I don't know," he answered. "But they must have been laced with something we ain't used to."

Milton lunged onto his right side, then began the process of clawing himself back to an upright position. He must have smoked more of that shit than I did. He looked like he was still fucked up.

"We need to walk," I said. "We need to get some food."

I offered my hand to help him, but he slapped it away.

"Get off me, punk. I got this."

He stood up, then immediately fell backwards. He tried to step back to catch himself, but his ankle twisted, and his leg crumbled beneath him. He fell rolling in the grass laughing like a child.

"Nigger, please," I said.

He stopped rolling and laughing, and offered his hand up for help. I grabbed his wrist; he grabbed mine. I leaned back and pulled as hard as I could. Slowly, he worked his legs under him and stood up.

"My nigger," he said, as a thank you. Then he got serious. "Folks don't like that expression, but it has meaning," he said. Then he said it again, "My nigger."

"Yeah," I answered as we began walking along the path by the water. "It means we both niggers."

"No," he said. "It's deeper than that."

"How so?" I asked.

"It means," he began, "that we may be the lowest of the low to the outside world, but we are in this shit together, and we will deal with it together by the strength of our balls. 'Cause that's all we got. I got your back, and you got mine, like soldiers in a war."

"Yeah," I said, "I guess I can see that."

"But it means even more than that," he continued. "Years ago when I was in jail waiting to go to trial, some Chicago police officers came to question me about the charges against me. These detectives said they needed some information, but they clearly did not. They just had this race game they were playing. They wanted me to call them honky, and they would call me nigger. It was some kind of power trip they wanted to play." He paused for a moment, then said, "But I refused to play. Then they wanted to get all friendly. They started telling me how slick the game they were running was."

"I don't understand," I said.

"Police departments across the nation all have an unwritten law they run by."

"Namely?" I asked.

"Namely, don't arrest white people."

"What if they're doing something wrong?"

"Doesn't matter. Don't arrest them."

"And the Black cops go for that?" I asked.

"They have no option," he answered. "They either go for it, or find another job."

"It sounds like you're saying that the primary function of police departments nationwide is to protect white people from Black people."

"That's exactly what I'm saying."

"These clowns bragged about the control they had over Black officers. If a Black officer begins arresting white offenders," he continued, "two things happen. First, the arrestee gets a get-out-of-jail-free card. They slap him on the wrist, give him an I-bond, then send him home.

They never ever put him in the lockup with Black men. Secondly, they will tell the brother in clear terms not to arrest white people. No euphemisms. No beating around the bush. They will say it in plain English, 'don't arrest white people.'"

"And if he keeps doing it?"

"They reassign him to lockup duty, or set him up to catch a case or be killed. There is no middle ground."

"And this is happening across the country?"

"Coast to coast to coast," he confirmed. "They thought that having that level of control meant they could equate honkies with niggers. They wanted to have that same camaraderie like soldiers in the trenches. But it's not the same. Like soldiers, niggers are strong and proud and powerful," he said. "My calling them honkies would legitimize them, make honkies strong and powerful, too."

"What am I missing here?" I asked.

"The point is that we were having that conversation for only one reason, because they had badges. It was their badges that made them strong, not their balls. I told them that the same thing would happen to them that would happen to an arrestee that got sent to the lockup. There were three of them, and I told them that if they hadn't had those badges, they would have been sucking my dick. I *told* them as much."

"And they went for that?"

"They kicked my black ass is what they did." Milton laughed hardily. "Broke my nose and a couple of ribs. And they had this little black box with a crank on it that generated electricity when you turned the crank. They took pleasure in connecting the wires to my balls. I think they just wanted to see my dick like they had some kind of penis envy. They couldn't take their eyes off it. The freak bastards! But they got my point."

"Did they ever come back?"

"They never did. I guess they found somebody else to play their little power game with."

XV

"'Bonjee, man, you better be careful." Aba's tone was serious. "These motherfuckers is trying to set you *up*."

I was still shaken by the notion that *Das Innerste Feuer* might still be around and still looking for me. Was Aba talking about them or Menachem? How could he possibly know about the plan Menachem and I were concocting? But then, how could he possibly know about *Das Innerste Feuer*? I played the nut role.

"What?"

"Don't what me, motherfucker. I know what's up."

"I'm confused," I said.

"Okay, how about this?" Aba challenged. "How do you suppose I knew when and where to intercept you earlier today? You think I just happened to be there?"

Okay. Clearly, he was talking about recent events.

"Ezra put a bug in your apartment the day he was there."

"Ezra? Who is Ezra?"

"We heard you make the call to Gray Line tours."

"Who is Ezra and who is this we?"

Waiting for Aba's answer, I began looking around his apartment. It was spare. One couch across from a window that looked out onto a vacant lot with scattered debris from a demolition project. There was a table, scratched and well-worn, at one end of the couch. There was a folding chair in front of the window a little off center and angled towards the door. The floor was a bare grey tile.

"So," I asked again, "Who is Ezra and who is this we you mention?"

Aba looked at me. He looked away out the window for a long moment as if to see how much debris remained to be removed, then looked at me again.

"We are the Original Order of the Sphinx," he said. "We have a creed that we live by, 'Know, Dare, Will and Keep Silent.'"

My knees buckled. I could feel my breath growing shallow. I remembered with crystal clarity the day I ran upstairs when I was sixteen, and found that Grandma Daughter had left one of her books on the table in the living room open to a page with a picture of the Egyptian Sphinx on it. I had been fascinated by it. It was a drawing rather than a photograph, and I had been struck by the Africanness of the nose and lips. They were thick like mine. The caption read:

On the Egyptian Sphinx,
    the   human   head   represents   intelligence   and

knowledge;

the lion's claws, daring and action;

the bull's loins, will power, perseverance and labor;

the eagle's folded wings, silence.

Hence the quaternary of the magi:

KNOW, DARE, WILL, KEEP SILENT.

After Grandma Daughter died, I looked through her things for that book, but I never found it. And though I came to understand the meaning of the quaternary of the magi, I was surprised to hear it now. I began to wonder if there might be some hidden meaning to it all.

I eased my way over to the couch, and sat down. I feigned composure, because I didn't want Aba to know . . . anything. But the question nagging at the back of my mind was, could there have been a connection between Grandma Daughter and the Original Order of the Sphinx?

Aba went on, "A lot of punk motherfuckers out there think they know about the sphinx. A lot of spy and law enforcement agencies use the name. But they punks! They don't know shit."

"Spies are not magicians," I said.

"Yeah," Aba said, "they just *think* they are."

"So what about Ezra?" I asked. "Who is that?"

"Ezra works for the Israeli government."

"And?"

"And he and the people he works with are looking for a scapegoat."

"And?" I was becoming impatient.

"That scapegoat is to be you."

I was even more confused, so I continued the nut role.

"A scapegoat for what?" I asked.

"I know what you are planning," he answered.

"I'm not planning anything."

"Why are you doing this?" he asked.

"Doing what?" I asked back. Then I said, "If you know what I'm planning, tell *me* what it is. And who the fuck is Ezra?"

"Look, man, I'm trying to help you. Ezra came to your house the other day, and was there for hours."

"The only person who came to my . . . .." I had to stop myself. Clearly, Ezra was Menachem. But this shit was getting too deep. I began to wonder who Aba was tracking, me or Menachem. Then I said, "Look, man, I ain't planning a motherfucking thing. And if this Ezra is planning something, I don't know about it."

His response was, "Hey, man, I'm just trying to help."

We went back and forth in that vein for another few minutes, then realizing he wasn't going to get any more information from me than he already had, Aba changed the topic.

"So how has business been?" he asked.

"Been good," I answered, "real good." Then I said, "But let's not talk about that. Tell me more about the Original Order of the Sphinx."

He paused for a long moment, then said, "I've got something I need to show you."

He disappeared through a doorway at the far end of the room. I could hear him opening what sounded like a cupboard. Or maybe it was a chest of drawers. He returned, and casually handed me a book. The corners were well-worn, and many of the pages were dog-eared. The cover was a pale tan bordering on a yellowish cream. The title read: The Original Order of the Sphinx. I couldn't tell who it was by, because that part of the cover had been taped over with silver duct tape in order to repair it.

"This is the book," he said. "It explains everything."

I fanned through the pages with my thumb to get a feel for the paper. I did that a couple of times just to see how much of the text had been highlighted. On the third time through, I noticed that there were a few pictures in the middle of the text. Then I saw it. But it flipped by so quickly that I wasn't sure. So I stopped fanning through, and flipped back one page at a time until there it was, the exact same image of the sphinx with the exact same caption.

"Where did you get this book?" I asked. I had to struggle to keep my voice level.

Aba seated himself in the chair on the other side of the room from me. He sat back and crossed his legs. He smoothed the burgundy fabric on his knee.

"I ran across it in a used bookstore in Old Town about thirty years ago," he answered. "I had been in Piper's Alley a hundred times, and had never seen this store. Then one day, there it was. And the proprietor was a creepy little man, real skinny with a beak nose and skin so thin you could almost see his skull through it. He wore an ill-fitting, black suit. Reminded me of an undertaker. I was flipping through it, and he came up behind me and said that I was going to need it one day. So I bought it. I thought about the sale on the way home, and realized I had been scammed. I tried to return it the next day, but the store was already gone. A sign in the window read, 'For rent.' Strangest thing. This book has changed my life."

I didn't say it to Aba, but this book also changed *my* life.

"And you've kept it all this time?" I asked.

"Yeah," he answered. "It's the only copy I've ever seen."

I closed the book, and turned it over and over slowly. I smelled it. I imagined that I could smell the lotions and potions Grandma Daughter had in her room before she died. I opened the book to the first page, and I read the first passage.

> He is that He is, and We are His Children. Therefore, We are that We are. We are the Alpha and the Omega, the Morning and the Evening Stars. None have come before Us; none shall come after. There was only Us in the Beginning; there will be only Us in the End.

I tried to remember whether or not Grandma Daughter had mentioned anything about the Original Order of the Sphinx when I was a child. I drew a blank. I remembered her face clear as crystal. In particular, I remembered her eyes. She had the kind of eyes that were not afraid to look at people. Her eyes held power. Most people who looked her in the eye looked away after only a few moments. But I remembered nothing about the Original Order of the Sphinx.

I turned a few more pages into the book, and read more.

They came from the north, from Scotland. They were Saxons fleeing William the Conqueror. They were loyal to Malcolm III and his son, David I. They designed and built the Dunfermline Abbey. They were builders of the first rank. They knew the building trade secrets that had been passed down from generation to generation.

I flipped more pages, and continued.

They came to Egypt aboard Royal African Company ships. They were confused by the design of the pyramids. The pyramids were nothing like anything they had ever built. They could not understand. They wanted to know, but they did not. They needed to conceal the fact that someone knew building techniques they did not know. So they claimed to know the unknown. They called His secrets their secrets, their rites. Their biggest secrets were that their secret rites were stolen, and that they didn't know the real secrets at all. They replaced the true secrets with secrets of their own. They feigned true knowledge to hoodwink the world.

I remembered that Grandma Daughter had secrets. She would palm herself as an ambulance or fire truck would roar by. It was like Catholics crossing themselves, but different. She would put the palm of her right hand to her forehead, then to her heart, then to her navel. She would say that the noise upset her stomach and gave her a headache, but I knew it wasn't true because the noise never bothered anybody else. In fact, nobody else would even notice the noise if the sirens were at a distance. But Grandma Daughter always heard them and always palmed herself. She later told me she palmed herself to acknowledge God's intervention on Earth. I now wondered if that was a ritual from the Original Order. I was tempted to ask Aba about palming to see if he knew anything about it. I decided not to.

I flipped past the pages of pictures in the middle, nearly to the end, and continued on.

The image of He that is, the builder of the

pyramids, also confounded them. He did not look like them. So they defiled His image, broke off His nose, so they could claim that the image was one of them. Now the deception was complete. They then sold His Children as slaves for enormous profit. The English royal family is awash with blood money from the sale of millions of His Children.

I began flipping through the pages again. The unmistakable scent of Grandma Daughter wafted up at me. All of a sudden, I could see her face with its shiny cheeks, its long, angular nose and flaring nostrils, its wide, thick lips that turned up slightly at the corners with an inborn smile. This was her book! But how could that be? It was impossible. This had to be a copy.

I kept my cool, but I began to wonder how there could be an Original Order of the Sphinx if Aba had the only copy of their bible. His story didn't wash.

"Where did you say you got this?" I asked.

I reached the end of the book. I closed it, and turned it over and over again slowly. I tried to piece together the parts of possible scenarios that could end with Grandma Daughter's book being in Aba's possession.

"I told you," he said. "I got it at a little bookstore in

Old Town."

"I wonder how it got there," I mused.

I opened the back cover, and my pulse surged. There was a picture glued to the last page, a picture I had seen years earlier. I recalled that at that time, the picture was so old, I could barely make out any details. I was having the same problem now, only worse, because the picture was in worse condition now. I was only able to recognize what was in the picture because I had seen the picture before.

For just a moment, I was back in Germany, hearing Ruby, my wife at the time, scream, "Anna, he knows," after this very picture popped out of the brass head of a cane she had tried to hit me with. I didn't want to remember how much I had loved her, how Anna had turned her against me, how Anna had killed her in her attempt to kill me. I pushed the thoughts from my head. I didn't want to remember that I didn't know what she had thought I knew. That was a long time ago. I forced myself to concentrate on the photograph.

The image in the picture resembled the head of a deceased Egyptian pharaoh, but it was different somehow. The headdress wasn't the same, wasn't quite Egyptian. Or maybe it was very early Egyptian. I hadn't been sure the first time I saw it, and I wasn't sure now.

I had squinted my eyes to try to recognize a clue. I did the same now, but it did not help. Then I recalled that it wasn't the headdress I had been recognizing. I had been and was now recognizing the face. At that time, the face was older, much older. And drawn. The person looked almost exactly like I had imagined I would look in fifty years. But now that I was older for real, the person in the picture looked almost exactly like me. It was blurry, but it was me. I closed the book.

"I've got to go," I said.

"We're not done talking," Aba protested.

"I've got to *go*," I said again.

Aba extended his hand for the book. I wanted to keep it, but I couldn't think of how to do that without revealing more than I wanted to reveal. I gave it to him, and lunged headlong for the door.

*****

"So, how did it go?" Ariella asked, "Did you have your meeting?"

We were back on her bike, riding along a boulevard I did not recognize as having driven on in order to get to the meeting in the first place. It seemed as if I was seeing all the buildings we were passing for the first time. All the landmarks we passed seemed new.

Or maybe I was merely distracted by having seen Grandma Daughter's book again for the first time in– what?– nearly forty years? Maybe it was the question that nagged at the back of my consciousness. How could it possibly be the same book?

"Turn around," I told Ariella. "We've got to go back."

"Why?" she asked.

"Turn the fuck around!"

She did not like it, but she did as I told her. I'm not sure why. She certainly did not have to, because there was nothing I could do to her. I told her to forget about the surveillance cameras, forget about the disguise and to take me straight to the address.

Once there, I hopped off the bike and barged straight up the stairs to the front door of Aba's apartment. I don't know what possessed me, but I didn't bother to knock. I simply turned the knob, and to my surprise, the door opened. The bigger surprise was that the apartment was empty. The couch was there, but not the chair in front of the window. I went through the rest of the apartment, and it looked as if no one lived there. Maybe there was nothing there in the first place. I hadn't bothered to check on my first visit.

I barged out with the same intensity I had as I barged

in. I needed to talk to Menachem.

I hopped onto the back of the bike, and Ariella sped off along that same stretch that I did not recognize before. Now, a few things were familiar, a cell phone store, a restaurant.

Maybe she was mad at me, but Ariella seemed to be driving recklessly, dodging in and out of traffic. I was about to say something to her about it when she ran a stop sign, and clipped a woman's baby carriage. The buggy only rocked a little, but the woman was livid. I couldn't understand what she was saying, but Ariella stopped to try to console her. She wouldn't be consoled. From what I could gather, she called the police. The two of them shouted back and forth for the entire four or five minutes until the police arrived.

I began to get nervous. The last thing I needed was to be taken to the police station. The women shouted at each other and at the officer. I kept my distance over by the bike. Then, silently, a black taxi pulled up next to me. It was a minivan with an automatic sliding door. The driver nodded for me to get in. It was the elf. He closed the door as we pulled away.

"How did you find me?" I asked.

"I've been following you."

"But why?"

"Because I know who you are."

We were only a short distance from my apartment building, so we arrived in fewer than three minutes. They seemed like an eternity. I wanted to ask him who he thought I was, but I couldn't be sure I could trust him. Getting that card at Caesarea turned everything weird. Maybe I should not have even gotten into the car.

As we pulled to a stop, he said, "Here you go. Safe and sound." I half expected him to get out and open the door for me as he had done before. Instead, he opened the automatic sliding door using a button on the dashboard. I stepped one foot out, then asked, "Who do you think I am?"

"You have come to rescue us," he answered. "You are God." His tone was matter-of-fact. There was no wonder in his voice. In his mind, he was just stating a fact.

For me, everything was changing. A flood of emotion rushed over me. Apprehension, curiosity, uncertainty, trepidation, abject fear, then slowly acceptance.

I recalled Frieda asking Lillian, *'Was ist mit Dir los?'* when Lillian realized who she thought I was.

"Quiet, child," Lillian had answered. "This is neither the time nor the place to explain."

"I am not God," I said to the elf. As much as anything, my response was a reflex, an answer I had long since become accustomed to giving in response to this situation.

He smiled that elven smile and closed the door. He drove away.

XVI

"His name is Mas Brownlee," Menachem said. "He's a CIA mole."

I had wanted to ask him if he knew anything about *Das Innerste Feuer*, but I didn't dare. Instead, I asked about Aba.

"But what's he doing here?"

"He's spying on the contingent of Black people who immigrated here from America."

"But why? Are folks here planning something?"

"That doesn't matter. He's been here for years keeping tabs on what they are thinking. The CIA recruited artists of all stripes to spy on their colleagues beginning years ago."

"Are there lots of artists here?" I asked.

"Not really," he answered, "and the ones who are aren't especially politically active."

"So what's he doing?"

"I've already told you more than you are cleared to know."

I couldn't think. My thoughts seemed so muddled. Why would Aba be tracking Black folks? And why would Aba be in the CIA? It didn't fit. Something was wrong. I couldn't help wondering whether *Das Innerste Feuer* was behind any of this.

"I've got a problem," I said. "The job is off."

Menachem was genuinely surprised. His breathing became irregular. I could see his pulse beating in his neck. He was beginning to flush.

"But everything is planned," he said. "I've got money, passports, tickets."

"For who?" I asked.

"For you!" he said. "The game is on. Benjamin is on the move."

"What!" I couldn't believe what I was hearing.

"Benjamin is leaving Tel Aviv tonight," he said, "and he will be back in three days."

"Who planned all of this?" I asked.

"We did." He stopped and corrected himself. "*I* did," he said.

I couldn't postpone asking this question. Too many things were not adding up.

"Who's Ezra?" I asked.

"I'm Ezra."

I had expected him to feign ignorance. When he didn't, I was taken aback.

"Ezra is the name the CIA knows me by," he continued.

"Is Menachem your real name? Or is Ezra?"

"My real name is not important. What is important is that you've got to make this shot, and make it count. You won't get a second chance."

"Why should I do this?" I asked him.

"There is much that you do not know," he said.

"Start filling me in," I demanded.

Menachem sat with his head bowed down in his hands for a long moment. "You don't have a need to know," he said.

"Aba is my friend," I said. "I've known him for years. I trust him. And he says that I cannot trust you. Now, where do you think that leaves you?"

He looked up at me. "I'm going to tell you something that is so secret, you and I both will be dead within five minutes if you divulge it. Is that clear?"

"It's clear," I said.

"Mas Brownlee is the patsy that is going to take the fall for step three of the plan to destroy America."

"Step three? What were the first two steps?"

"Those steps were American-sponsored, false-flag attacks on American soil."

"I know," I said. "911 was step one."

"911 was step two," he corrected. "The Alfred P. Murrah Federal Building in downtown Oklahoma City on April 19, 1995, was step one."

"That was not a false-flag attack," I corrected.

"Yes, it was," he insisted, "and Timothy McVeigh was the patsy."

"Com' on, man," I said. "Timothy McVeigh was a patriot!"

"Timothy McVeigh was working for the U.S. Army," he said. "Why do you suppose he never bothered to cover his tracks? He rented the truck in his own name, for Christ sake!"

"So, he made a mistake," I countered.

"And he surrendered to that officer because he had expected the army to bail him out. Instead, the army let him take the fall."

Now, I was *really* confused. And apparently, my confusion was evident on my face. Menachem continued with his narrative as if more details would clear things up for me.

"The ATF," he said, "at the direction of the CIA, planted charges on major support beams in the Murrah building. At the time of the blast, the ATF office was empty. After the blast, they showed up and played the part of rescuing heros."

It must have been obvious that these added details didn't do the trick. So he offered more.

"Think about the similarities between the Murrah job

and the Twin Towers job," he said. "In both cases, the purported cause of the destruction wasn't big enough to cause the actual damage done. In the Murrah case, that one little truck simply was not big enough to cause that much damage. Besides, the blast pattern was all wrong. And in the nine-one-one case, there was building seven."

I was listening, but my head was swimming. There was a humming in my ears that I was tempting to focus on rather than to continue to listen to Menachem. From somewhere, the notion came to me that concentrating on the humming would somehow make everything clear.

"In both cases," he continued, "either no real investigation was done, or the investigation was done by the same people who committed the crime, namely, the U.S. government."

He stopped. Apparently, he thought that everything should be clear for me by now. He waited for my reaction.

"So what is step three?" I asked.

"That's the part that can get us killed," he stressed. "That's the part that nobody is supposed to know."

"So how do *you* know?" I asked him.

"Benjamin has contacts in the CIA who have access to this information. I have access to Benjamin."

"He trusts you like that?" I asked.

"Of course not," he answered. "But I'm in a position to catch snippets of conversations or see doodles or whatever, and put two and two together. Mind you, even Benjamin's CIA contact doesn't have the whole picture, because nobody at the CIA does, unless you are very high up and very well connected. Everybody gets to know only so much, only as much as is needed to do a small portion of the overall job."

"So what is the third step?"

"Bear in mind that steps one and two drove a fear in the American mind that the American public is still wrestling with. Meanwhile, municipal police units are being outfitted with military grade vehicles and munitions. Once that upgrade in equipment is complete, step three will happen."

"And step three is?"

Menachem hesitated. "I don't know exactly," he said. "But the plans are already worked out in detail, and sitting on the shelf waiting for the right moment. It will be another terrorist attack." He flexed the index and middle fingers of both hands in the air to indicate that terrorist attack should be in quotes. "And it will be huge. A dirty bomb in a small city. A dam explosion. Something where the body count will be higher than the Twin Towers, somewhere around 10,000 casualties.

That's when civil liberties will be suspended for good, and the police will become units of the U.S. government to keep the peace. That's when what is left of democracy in America will be dead forever."

"And Brownlee will take the fall?"

"He doesn't know it yet, but, yes, he will take the fall. It will all be blamed on him, just like the Murrah job was blamed on Timothy McVeigh and Terry Nichols."

"And the Masons?" I asked.

"The Masons and billionaires around the world are the brains behind the CIA. They are the hidden hand. That's why killing billionaires is so important." He interlaced his fingers and pushed his palms out in front of him. Several of his knuckles snapped. "So, now," he said, "I've got this 50 caliber rifle, hundreds of thousands dollars, passports from Belize, Liberia and Guyana, tickets out of Israel for all those passports, and information on where Benjamin will be in three days with a clear shot. Are you in?"

He looked at me and blinked histrionically.

"How are you going to pin this on Brownlee?" I asked. I had to work to keep from calling him Aba.

"That information is above your pay grade."

"Then I guess you need to give me a promotion. That is, of course, if you want the job done."

He thought about it, then said, "Nobody in the CIA has the whole picture. The folks who have him over here spying on American expatriates don't know that another group within the CIA is using this trip to link him to various terrorist organizations."

"One hand lacking knowledge of what the other hand is doing?" I asked.

"Exactly," he answered. "That is a way of life in the CIA. One group is setting him up to be a hero, while the other group is building a portfolio to present to the public showing how he trained for years to kill Americans."

He rubbed his hand several times across his forehead again, then said, "Brownlee is playing you for a fool."

"How so?" I asked.

"He pretends to be your friend, but how well do you know him?"

"He helped me get my first contract in the business."

"Yes, but did you know him before that?"

I thought about it, and had to admit that I hadn't known Aba long before then at all.

"Brownlee is a trained assassin. He uses poisons, some of which induce heart attacks."

"What's your point?"

"Didn't your mother die of a heart attack?"

"How do you know that?" I asked. "I thought you told me your guys couldn't find anything on me."

"I did tell you that. But that was before I needed you to do this job."

"How much do you have on me?"

Years earlier I had called Mama from a subway phone while I was in New York City. It was Christmas. The following spring, she died. I had called her just to let her know I was still doing fine. The woman who answered the phone told me Mama had had a heart attack the week before, and had died in Cook County Hospital. She knew of no next of kin. I hated not attending her funeral, but I knew Anna's people would be there, too. I began to wonder whether or not Aba was one of Anna's people.

"I don't know a lot about you," Menachem answered. "But I know that Brownlee has a diary or book of some sort that his handlers think is pretty important. I don't know what it is, but they think it gives Brownlee some kind of advantage over you."

So that was how he did it. That was how he got Grandma Daughter's book. He found it in Mama's apartment after he killed her. Now I knew Menachem's story was true. I had to get it back.

"He does have a book that belongs to me," I said. "Get that book for me, and I'm in."

Menachem smiled, and I noticed for the first time that he had a pronounced overbite. I found myself wondering how he could bite his food given the gap between his upper and lower teeth.

"Done," he said. His smile broadened. "Consider it done."

XVII

Chicago was cold when I got back. It was January. It felt good to be back in my apartment. It felt good to see things around me that were familiar. My books. My swords on the walls. My drapes. My black leather couch. My aquarium, empty now because I drained it before leaving for Israel. The living room still smelled of sandalwood and linseed oil. But I couldn't shake it. I couldn't shake the elf. I couldn't shake *Das Innerste Feuer*. On the planes back, and in the airports during layovers, I was paranoid. Everybody I saw turned into Anna Müller a.k.a. Mighty Red, the woman who tried to kill me years– decades– ago in Germany because of who she thought I was. I could see her just as clearly now as the day we first met her.

Mighty Red was big-boned and muscular like an athlete. She had short, heavy legs, and she walked with a short, heavy stride. She had huge breasts. When she walked, she led with her breasts like a ram leading with its horns. Her face was gentle, though. It was square and had more angles at the jaw than would normally be found in a woman's face. But her thin lips turned easily into a soft smile, and her smooth skin, upturned little nose and soft, friendly eyes that squinted when she smiled made me think of her more than once in the beginning as Mrs. Santa Claus.

That image was so misleading. The woman was a snake. According to Lillian, she had worked with the Nazis for years on different kinds of mind-altering drugs. But more importantly, she was a longtime member of *Das Innerste Feuer*. She was the one who had sent the dwarf to shoot me at Rainbow Beach. My paranoia was not without justification. The woman clearly wanted me dead.

The trip back was long and hard. I slept all day the day I arrived home. There's something about being back in your own bed. Being up on the morning of the first full day of not being jet-lagged felt like a new beginning. Anything was possible. Anything could happen. But first, I needed to clear my head.

I turned on the flat-screen to CNN. They were covering the Benjamin shooting. Israel was in some state of high alert. I turned the sound down, and went into the kitchen to get some food. Grandma Daughter's picture was still there on the table where I had left it before I took off for Tel Aviv.

I rustled up some grits with butter and cheese and a couple of soy sausages. I sat down at the table to eat.

From my kitchen, I could see the flat-screen in the living room. There was some woman with blonde hair talking to some clown with a bow tie and horn rimmed glasses. I looked down at my plate to stir the butter and cheese into the grits. When I looked up again, there was a picture of Aba with words scrolling across the bottom. I hopped up and dashed in to turn up the sound.

"This just in," the reporter announced. "Mas Brownlee has been captured and charged with the murder of Nathan Benjamin, the prime minister of Israel."

The report went on to say that Brownlee had been living in Israel for a number of years, and had been photographed casing various sites around Tel Aviv. They showed one of the pictures they captured of him sitting on a bench. But it wasn't him. It was me. I recognized the clothes the person in the picture was wearing. It was me with Aba's face superimposed over mine. The deception was superb. If I had not known that the picture was not Aba, there was nothing in the picture itself to give it away.

From Aba, the program switched to an interview with Abraham somebody. I missed the last name. But it was Menachem flapping at length about how Mas

Brownlee had acted on behalf of the PLO, and that Israeli authorities had been lucky that the culprit had made so many mistakes. He declared there would be massive retaliations. It was a great cover-up story. They then flashed a picture of Aba wearing his kufi, the same one he had worn the day he stopped me outside the bank in Tel Aviv. I began to wonder who the CIA would be targeting next to be the patsy for their upcoming 'terrorist attack.' I began to wonder if they could be considering me. I had to be careful.

Three days later, I received a box with a cell phone in it. The box was unmarked, and it was delivered to my apartment door by the building engineer. He said someone paid him 50 dollars simply to deliver a package within the building. When I asked who this someone was and what they looked like, he said, "Who knows? All I saw was the money."

The following day, I got a call on that phone. It was Menachem.

"So, Menachem-Ezra-Abraham," I said, "how's it going?"

"Cut the shit," he responded. "We need to talk."

I wondered what could be so urgent. The job was done. I had my money. Everything was fine.

"This is a secure phone," he said, "so we can talk

freely."

Shi-i-it! There was no way I was going to talk freely on this or any other phone with him or anybody else. But I said, "Cool, what's up?"

"The Masons pretend to promote order out of chaos. But in truth, they promote chaos out of order."

"Menachem," I said, "is that what I should call you? Is that your name?"

"Menachem is my real name."

"Okay, Menachem it is," I said, "What the fuck are you talking about?"

"I'm talking about Masonic control of the planet."

"I thought we decided to go after billionaires."

"Yes," he responded, "we did. But the reason we cannot find the Masons is because they promote chaos out of order."

"But, so what? That knowledge changes nothing."

"It changes everything," he said, "because now we can determine which ones to go after first."

"Why does it matter?" I asked.

"It matters because some billionaires are merely greedy. Others are actively enslaving us. It is the ones who are actively enslaving us that we need to attack first."

"I'm not seeing the difference," I said. "Chaos out of

order tells me nothing."

"I'll take care of that part of it," he said. "I'm going to research who has done what, and why they should die first. This is, after all, going to be a long-term project."

"Great," I said, "you do that. But in the meantime, I'm going to be researching and picking targets as best I can."

"Fine," he said. "I'm going to see that all my communications to you get delivered by way of diplomatic pouch the way that phone got there."

"I look forward to it."

"We need a way to recruit assassins," he said. He was clearly musing. "There are a lot of billionaires in the world." Then he added, "Destroy that phone and hide the debris. I'll send you a new one each time we need to talk."

XVIII

I wanted to see Brit. I wanted to fuck Brit, but I knew that would be too dangerous. I didn't know if I would be able to resist wanting to wallow in her blood. I could still see her face morph into Kelly's face, and I could still hear Kelly calling me Daddy. I needed to find someone else.

I remembered the name of a dungeon Brit had told me about shortly after we began to get close. She told me where it was, but we never went there. She didn't like being kinky in public. Hard to believe given the way we repeatedly freaked off in the back of her truck. Granted, the windows were tinted, but she made enough noise that anyone passing by would know what we were doing.

I checked out the dungeon's website. It was called the Leather Lily, and it's logo was a series of three lilies with a drop of blood at the tip of each petal. It reminded me of Easter, and it felt strange to be looking for a fuck buddy on a website with Jesus's blood as part of its logo. It made an already perverted act seem more perverted yet.

The website had posted a series of events, and a registration form to fill out in order to get the exact address. I picked the event that offered a class on whipping, filled out the form, and hit the enter button.

I already had a decent whipping technique, but I figured I could always use some new pointers.

The place was hard to find, even with the exact address. I had expected a door with numbers. Instead, the front door was around the side of the building and down a full flight of stairs. I felt almost as if I were trespassing, because the stairs were not even visible from the street side of the edifice. I pushed open the heavy steel door, and approached the greeter. He was an elderly brother with serious pock scares all over his face. He was cheerful as he had me fill out a form that stated that I would be entering at my own risk. The Leather Lily would not be responsible for any injuries I received while there. I couldn't help wondering if more than a whipping class was going on here tonight. The event was free, but there was a suggested donation, if I wanted to make one, of ten dollars. He buzzed me in.

It took a minute for my eyes to adjust to the light. The walls were all painted black, and there were dim lanterns in all the corners. A couple of ornate chandeliers cast an ambient glow. The place was actually creepy, like Dracula's castle. Or maybe that was the intended effect. A couple of couches and chairs in some muted color rested against one wall. There was another small, striped couch against the far adjacent wall. The opposite wall was covered with lashes and whips and chains and clasps and prods. A huge dildo adorned a small table like a trophy. It had its own little lantern. I couldn't resist the urge to look around for an equally big plaster of Paris pussy. There wasn't one.

"Welcome, welcome." The voice was behind me. "You can sit right over here."

I turned in response.

"I'll stand, thank you," I said.

"Suit yourself. My name is Charles. They call me Chip-the-Whip. You're new here."

"I am," I said. "Just here to pick up some pointers, some techniques."

"Good," Chip said, "we'll be starting demonstrations shortly."

After Chip left, I found a seat on one of the couches. I had never been in a dungeon before. I was fascinated with the openly kinky sexuality on display. I had been in gentlemen's clubs many times. The Million Dollar Saloon came to mind. That was where on a contract in Toronto I had almost fallen in love with Jasmine, a Jamaican beauty, who showed me enough of her pussy that I thought at the time that I would be in love with her forever. But this place was out-the-box! Here, people just out-and-out fucked.

I looked further around. There was a small bar in the adjacent corner serving strictly non-alcoholic beverages. The bar looked old. I imagined it had been rescued from an abandoned building or something. I made a donation and got a lemonade. The man tending the bar was stark naked except for a dog collar around his neck. He looked to be around fifty. He was stoop-shouldered with tufts of hair growing across his back. There was a small cage chained to his dick and balls, and the chain led between his legs to something stuck in his ass. I wanted for all the world to ask what it was, but the instructions on the website admonished against asking too many questions. Apparently, what happened in the dungeon stayed in the dungeon.

I sat sipping my lemonade, and checking out the other patrons. To the left, there was an island of chairs where three women and two men gathered together discussing the differences between a thud and a sting. I remembered that Brit had always preferred stings to thuds. She liked the way they made her nerves tingle. That's why I gave her so many thuds. I wanted her to feel the pain deeper inside her body.

In the far corner, a man dressed in a black business suit stood behind a naked woman chained to a St. Andrew's cross. She was chained spread-eagle with a fox tail hanging from her ass. The man snatched the fox tail from her ass, and she voiced a short yelp. Her body tensed from the pain. The man grabbed her hair, and pulled her head back. He whispered something in her ear. She sniffed, and reluctantly nodded yes. He unzipped his fly, and inserted his dick where the fox tail had been. She angled her ass up as high as she could in total submission to his demand. Gentlemen's clubs were never like this.

Off to the right, Chip bound the wrists of a naked, twenty-something young man to another St. Andrew's cross. He then bound the man's ankles. The young man was plump like a cherub, and had small feet and even toes with flaming red lacquer on the nails. He probably thought that made him look more feminine. It didn't. He just looked like a man with painted toenails. Or maybe it made him *feel* more feminine. The young man gave Chip feedback as to how tight the restraints should be. Chip ignored him, and made the ropes as tight as *he* wanted them to be. When he was done, Chip turned and faced the open room.

"Okay," he said. "Let's get this show started."

The thud-versus-sting crowd meandered to this side of the room. The man in the black suit took his dick out of the woman's ass, and zipped his fly. He scurried across the floor leaving her chained in place. I wondered when he planned to wash his dick.

The bartender wiped the bar counter, and rearranged some glasses. He reached around to adjust the plug in his ass, then went back to arranging the glasses. I looked at my glass of lemonade. I wasn't sure whether or not I wanted to sip from it again.

"This is Johnny," Chip said. "He goes by Testosterpussy on Fetlife. He was gracious enough to volunteer to be my boy-toy for tonight."

Chip went on about different kinds of whips and different techniques for different results. He had six whips on display next to where Johnny was bound. He pointed to each in turn, and talked briefly about its merits. He then selected a short, single-tail whip. It was hard to see its details from this distance and in this light, but it looked to be burgundy snake skin. It was about two, maybe two and a half feet long with an eight or nine inch stiff handle. There was a loop at the handle for slipping around the wrist. The tip was a three inch piece of leather in that same color. It was truly a work of art.

Chip stepped away from the whips, and moved next to Johnny. He made Johnny kiss the it. Twice. Then he stood a few paces behind Johnny. Chip looked like a computer geek, short, skinny, pale, with a receding chin, and wire-rim glasses. He looked like a character from a revenge-of-the-nerds movie. That impression immediately changed as he began whirling the whip in a figure-8 motion, turning his wrist deftly with each arc. The whip cutting through the air was surprisingly quiet.

Twirling that whip, Chip looked confident and sure of himself. He took half a step closer to Johnny, just close enough for Johnny to feel the wind of the whip as its tip passed his skin. Johnny's body began to quiver in anticipation.

Just then, Chip changed the motion of the whip to one that was horizontal back and forth, back and forth. He stepped in another half step so that the tip of the whip caught Johnny right on his butt, one side then the other, over and over again. The strikes were barely audible. Johnny tensed at the first few licks of the whip, and audibly hissed as he drew air in through his teeth. After a few passes back and forth, he relaxed and slumped into his bonds.

Chip worked the whip down Johnny's butt and half way down his thighs. Then he worked slowly back up. After a few seconds, Chip changed back to the figure-8, and began lashing Johnny across his shoulder blades, never hard enough to draw blood, but always hard enough to leave a red mark.

Then Chip changed back to the level horizontal pattern, this time across Johnny's upper back, over and over and over again. Johnny was so relaxed, I began to wonder whether or not he was even still alive. I remembered Brit lapsing into subspace like that as I beat her, but she never appeared to completely pass out. Johnny was all the way gone.

After ten or so minutes, Chip abruptly stopped. He placed the whip back next to the others, and picked up a paddle that I had not even noticed was there. He must have had it lying under the whips. It looked like a ping-pong paddle, only bigger. He moved slowly next to Johnny. Standing there together, they made an incongruent couple. Chip was half a head shorter than Johnny, and Johnny was heavier than Chip by 50 pounds. It looked as if Johnny should have been the one in control. But clearly, he was not. Chip was in full control. I could hear him ask Johnny if he wanted to stop. Johnny shook his head violently, no. Chip told him to prove it by kissing the paddle. Johnny did as he was told. Johnny kissed the paddle a dozen times. Then he told Johnny to kiss him. Chip stuck his tongue deep into Johnny's mouth, and Johnny took it in. When Chip removed his tongue, Johnny slumped back into his bonds. He looked to be in a deep trance.

Chip worked him with the paddle for a total of about 30 minutes, hitting in the exact same places he had hit him with the whip. When he was done, he unbuckled Johnny, who then slumped all the way to the floor. Chip snapped his fingers, and the bartender brought over a large beverage. Chip knelt down to Johnny, and caressed his head. He made Johnny drink long from the beverage. Then Chip lowered Johnny's head back to the floor. Johnny lay there in the fetal position for a solid fifteen minutes before he began to revive. During that time, Chip would check on him to make sure he was okay. On the third check, Chip helped him to sit upright, and gave him some more to drink. Johnny drained the glass, and smiled at Chip. "Thanks," he said. "That was wonderful."

By now, all the play sessions were over. The man in the black suit and the woman with the fox tail were at the bar sipping sodas. The thud-versus-sting crowd was broken up into various couples. One of the couples was on the small, striped couch against the far adjacent wall, not far from the trophy dildo. He had his hand deep in her pussy, and she was thrusting her hips forward to get it in deeper. I had to look away, because it reminded me that I no longer had someone whose pussy I could stick my hand into.

Chip came over and sat next to me. I could smell that he was still sweaty from beating Johnny.

"So," he asked, "did you learn anything?" I imagined that I could smell Johnny on him as well.

"I did," I answered. "I learned a lot." My answer was genuine.

"I usually give folks who are interested a chance to try it out for themselves," he said. "But today, Johnny had about all he could take."

"I'm not sure I would have volunteered anyway," I said. "But I do appreciate the offer. Maybe next time."

"We're here if you need us," he said, and hefted himself off the couch. "There are a lot of folks here looking for good people to beat and fuck them."

"I'll bear that in mind," I said.

By now, it was time to leave. I had come hoping to meet someone, but that was not going to happen tonight. I gave a short wave to Chip and Johnny both now sitting at the bar, and headed for the steel exit door. Just as I reached for the knob, Chip shouted out to me.

"Before you go," he said, "let me show you our rope room."

The rope room was behind a black curtain on the far side of the exit door. I had scarcely noticed it. Chip pulled the curtain back allowing me to enter first.

Like the main room, the rope room was painted black and had low glowing lanterns placed in each corner. But this room was appointed differently. It had two large wooden scaffolds for tying and suspending people. I knew this because one of them supported the weight of a man who was tied with his arms behind his back, and his legs pulled apart by ropes fastened to two of the corner posts. His weight was being supported by latices of rope tied around his torso and looped over one of the four-by-four beams at the top of the scaffold. Like Johnny earlier, this man appeared to be in a meditative state. His eyes were half closed, and his breathing was slow and even. I began to wonder how it might feel to be suspended in that way.

The woman tying him up was completely engrossed in her work. There was something familiar about her, though. From behind, she looked like a boy, skinny with no ass. She was lashing a rope around the man's neck and looping it through a ring suspended from another one of the beams at the top. I guess it was because I didn't know what she was doing, but it looked to me like she was getting ready to lynch the man. And given his meditative state, he was cool with it. He completely trusted her. I imagined that it must take years to surrender that much of yourself to a person in that way.

Chip called the woman's name.

"Alice," he said, "there is someone I want you to meet."

The woman turned, and I saw why she looked familiar. Her hair was short now, and was dyed orange. But her dark almond eyes and her delicate round and flat face were the same except that the skin was weathered and sagged at the eyes and cheeks. I couldn't see her coloration because of the low lighting. I allowed myself to imagine that she was still the pale yellow I still remembered. She wore an outfit of black leather straps that covered next to nothing. The top was like a bra with no cups, and the bottom was like a jockstrap, also with no cup. Her breasts were the same as they had always been, small like over-sized nipples. Her pubic hair was shaved. The skin all over her body was leathery now. Clearly, she was older, too. But it was her, the woman who disappeared with no trace from a burning building over near Rainbow Park, the woman with whom I had believed I might spend the rest of my life, the woman who when I last saw her was carrying my child.

Chip looked at her expression, then looked at mine.

"Do you guys know each other?" he asked.

She said, "Jay."

I said, "Jiqin."

Chip was confused. "Jiqin?" He said, "I thought your name was Alice."

"It is Alice," she responded, "when I'm here in Wonderland."

I had to work to contain my glee at seeing her. There was so much I wanted to know. Where did she go? How was the baby? How did the fire get started? But all I could muster was, "How you doing?"

I remembered she had just told me she was pregnant. She wanted ice cream, and I had gone out to get some. When I got back, the house was on fire, and she and everybody in it were gone.

"How I'm doing is I'm pissed," she said. "And I have been for years."

Chip started visibly. "I guess you two *do* know each other." Then he said, "I think I'll leave you guys alone."

We watched Chip arrange the curtain back in place after leaving. Jiqin was about to speak, but I stopped her and looked over at the man hanging among the network of ropes. He was still in a trance.

"He's nobody," she said. "We're alone."

"Are you pissed at me?"

"Yes, at you!"

"Why?" I asked. "What did I do?"

"Because you left us."

"Left you?! You're the one who left! I got back and found the fucking house burning!"

Her demeanor instantly changed.

"I guess you want an explanation," she said.

"That would be nice," I answered.

I couldn't resist looking at her body. I wanted to see if she looked pregnant or had stretch marks or something or anything.

"The baby died," she said.

"Why did you leave? I thought we had something."

"We did," she said.

"So what happened?"

She stepped forward and put her arms around my neck. I tried to step back away from her, but she followed my every move. I had forgotten how well-trained she was. My back was against the wall after only about three steps.

"What happened?" I asked again.

She released me, and slid to her knees. She kowtowed to me. Being Chinese, this girl knew how to kowtow. Brit had a way of kowtowing without actually kowtowing. She would be on her knees with her forehead on the floor, but something in her demeanor told me she didn't really mean it, that she was putting on a front. Jiqin was different. She meant her kowtow.

"What happened?" I asked again.

"I burned the house down."

"Why?"

"I didn't believe you wanted the baby. I thought you abandoned us."

"What?!"

"I'm sorry," she said. She sank deeper yet into her kowtow. She was almost becoming a part of the floor.

"And where is the baby now?" I asked.

"The baby died. God is punishing me, because I miss the baby and you everyday." She said, "You took so long to get back, I thought you hated us."

"Hated you?! I loved you," I said. "I would have done almost anything for you."

"I'm sorry," she said. Her voice was quaking. Then she said, "I need for you to punish me. I need for you to humiliate me."

"Not here," I said.

"It has to be here; it has to be in public. It's the only way I can be cleansed of my guilt." She strained to get the words out.

"No," I said. "Stand up."

"You have to beat me," she said.

I told her to sit back, and she did. She sat back resting her weight on the heels of her feet. Her gaze was fixed on my fly. Just then, Chip walked it.

"Oh," he said, "I'm sorry."

He turned to leave, but she stopped him.

"Wait," she said. "I need for you to watch this. Go get everybody else."

"There's only a few folks left," Chip said.

"Get them."

Chip pulled the curtain open and shouted to the rest of the house, "Alice needs us to watch something."

"And have somebody cut Tony down," she said.

A handful of people straggled in. They seemed surprised. The naked bartender said, "I thought Alice was a Dom. What's she doing on her knees?"

Chip had the bartender and Johnny untangle the web of ropes suspending Jiqin's victim as she sat staring at my fly.

"Open it," she said.

I could see the emotion in her face. Water began to well up in her eyes. I told her, no.

"Please," she begged, "I need to do this."

I unzipped my fly, and she raised all the way up onto her knees. I unbuttoned my pants, and slid them down around my ankles. She leaned forward. I backed away a couple of inches.

"Please," she said again.

I angled myself closer in.

"I am so sorry," she said, her voice cracking. She took me into her mouth. I was soft, so she was able to get it all in. She began to sniff and cry as she sucked me.

She sucked for a while before I was able to say, "I forgive you."

A moan deep inside her slowly welled up. I could feel her moan resonating with a moan inside me. But I kept mine in. My dick slipped from her mouth as she buried her face in my pubic hair. She wept openly and without shame. She hugged me hard around my butt, forcing her face harder against my flesh.

After a few minutes, I pulled her hair so that her face angled up towards me.

"Do the Iron Body pose," I told her.

She leaned forward supporting her weight on her arms as if she were going to do push-ups.

I asked Chip if I could borrow his whip. He had one in his belt like Lash LaRue. He unbuckled it and handed it to me.

I moved around to Jiqin's feet, and used my foot to spread her feet apart. I stepped between her legs. I unfastened the thong she was wearing as well as that cupless bra. Now she was completely naked with her legs apart, supporting her weight on her outstretched arms. Her crying had subsided a little, but now it resumed. I could still feel the resonating of our moans in the pit of my stomach.

I stood up and whirled the whip like I had seen Chip whirl it earlier. I stepped in and popped her on the butt. She was crying openly again. I don't know what came over me, but remembering what we had, hearing her grieve for our dead baby, smelling her sweat and hair and ass, feeling her moan melding with my moan, I could feel my own tears welling up and my nose begin to run. Before long, I had images of her and Brit and Kelly flashing with free rein in my mind. I heard Kelly calling me daddy, and somehow it was the baby Jiqin and I had had calling out to me from the grave. Then Ruby and Ida memories flashed in. I was lost in a montage of completely unrelated life images. All the while, I whirled and whirled and whirled.

All at once, my whirls became my daddy's whirls. I was my daddy beating my mother, and Jiqin crying was my mother and Grandma Daughter crying because my daddy was beating them. I was him, and I hated him, and I hated myself. I wanted to beat *him* with the whip. And I did. I beat him and beat him and beat him. I could see his face, his almond-colored eyes, his small, turned-up nose and thin lips, looking almost like a white man. I slashed and slashed and slashed. I hated myself even more when I realized that I got my love for inflicting pain from him. I had become my father.

By the time I stopped, Jiqin's upper back and ass were covered with a crosshatch of lashes. I dropped the whip, and sank to my knees crying as hard as Jiqin had. I tried to stifle it, but I couldn't. I crawled over to her. Her arms were quivering from having to hold her weight for so long. I raised her up and hugged her and kissed her, and we cried together.

She broke our embrace, and leaned back on the hard floor. She spread herself inviting me to enter her.

"I don't know if I can," I said.

"We have to finish this," she said. "Please. I need for you to fuck me again even if it is only for a little while."

I played with my dick to get it hard. I crawled over her, and she directed it in. As I felt myself sinking into her, I heard the strangely satisfying release of a deep and haunting groan, low as if years of knowledge or wisdom or pain or something were being released. I thought it was Jiqin again, because it sounded so much like the resonating I had heard earlier. But there was something different about the way it vibrated. The vibrations were more intense, closer to the pit of my stomach, something that I might have heard come out of Grandma Daughter as she sat rocking and reading the Bible. That's when I realized that it was me. The groan came from deep inside of me.

XIX

"David Rockefeller?!" I wasn't sure I had heard him correctly. "You want us to kill *the* David Rockefeller?"

Menachem's voice was low and even. "Yes," he said, "*the* David Rockefeller."

"But he's an icon."

"All the more reason," he said. "He will be our poster boy. We are going to use him to show the world that the Rockefellers, Rothschilds, Morgans and other billionaire families can be stopped."

"I know," I said, "but why *him*?"

"Why *not* him? If we get him, the world, especially the world of billionaires, will get the message."

Earlier that day, when the building engineer had delivered this next box, he was especially happy. His wide smile exposed his tobacco stained teeth.

"I love it when you get these boxes," he had said. He flashed a 100 dollar bill. He blew me a kiss. I was tempted to duck.

It was another cell phone from Menachem with a note to call him. That's when he disclosed this impossible plan.

"But he'll have the best security in the world," I protested.

"You're a professional," he said. "You'll figure it out. And if not him, go for his son, David, Jr. Go for Jay. Or go for Nicholas. According to Aaron Russo, that asshole knew about 9-11 long before it happened. The Rockefellers helped finance it. There are hundreds of them out there. It doesn't matter which one you pick. Pick ten. Pick them all! Just make sure the deed is public."

"Why?" I asked.

"Because we want the billionaire-owned news media to cover it. We want all the billionaires in the world to feel the fear. We want them to fear every face they see in the street. We want them to fear their own staff, their maids, their butlers, their bodyguards. We want them to live in a constant state of soul-gnawing, agonizing fear."

"That's not going to work," I said.

"Why not?"

"Because they *won't* cover it for exactly the reason you want them *to* cover it."

"No," he said. "If they don't cover it, it'll be because they don't want copycats getting the message."

"Either way," I said, "it won't get covered."

"It doesn't matter," he said. "They don't rely on the media for their news anyway. They will each get the news *via* a phone call. So, make it public. Make it as public as the Kennedy assassination, and for the exact same reason, to send a world-wide message."

We chatted for a few more minutes about the situation in Israel since Benjamin's death, but my mind was elsewhere. For the first time, I was beginning to realize the full measure of what we were planning to do. Or maybe I was beginning to question the wisdom of the plan. It's funny how we rely on abstract philosophy when straight up reason doesn't fill in the gaps. I could feel myself grasping at loosely reasoned arguments to justify what some would posit was sheer madness. It was one thing to say, 'kill a billionaire.' It was an altogether different matter to give the billionaire a name.

Was I losing my resolve? Had I failed to correctly see the situation for what it was? I needed to clear my head. I needed to work up a sweat so I could get my vision back.

I hadn't had a good workout since before going to Israel. In fact, not since the house burned down with all my workout stuff in it. I went to the Clarendon Park Field House, because I knew they had a workout room there. It was wet with dark clouds bellowing overhead. I had to angle my head down in order to keep the sleet from pelting me directly in my face.

I got into my sweats, and stepped out onto the black,

rubber-padded floor. A row of treadmills sat along the wall to the right upon entering the room, and various machines for working different muscle groups sat in the middle of the floor. The rack with the free weights sat in the far corner. Several other men were in the room working out as well. I could smell the sweat in the air, and I knew that I missed it. I had been away from working out too long.

I found a couple of ten-pound weights on the rack. I set my feet, and began doing curls. Slowly at first, one arm, then the other. Then I remembered what my teacher, Master Yuen, had taught me about warming up first. Master Yuen had been Jiqin's uncle, and he was the one who trained me when we all lived in an abandoned apartment building on Seventy-seventh and Lakeshore Drive. He looked like he could have stepped out of a Fu Manchu Mystery, bald with a long, grey mustache. He was tiny and old, but he knew his stuff. He told me to never ever workout without stretching first. So I put the weights down and stretched.

I did head rolls to stretch the muscles in my neck, then shoulder rolls and pulls, wrist rolls and pulls, finger bends, trunk twists and bends, back leans, hip rolls in both directions, knee rolls in both directions, deep knee bends, ankle rolls and toe flexes and bends. When I picked the weights back up, I was good to go. I resumed doing curls, and my thoughts wandered as I alternated arm to arm.

I had always known that the monster that enslaves His Children had surveillance cameras and spies for eyes. It had armies and police departments for talons. Its teeth were central and major banks that the monster used to tear the economic flesh from the masses through income taxes and bank bailouts. The rules of engagement were its own laws. I knew that it could not be defeated by fighting it on its own terms. Its head had to be cleaved. Its head consisted of the super rich. Kill the super rich, and the monster will die! *That* was why to kill a billionaire. Or so I had always thought.

I did two sets of 50 curls on both arms. It felt good to be exercising again. I alternated the bicep curls with hammer curls. Back in the day, I would have done 300, 400, maybe 500 of these. Now, a hundred was all I could muster. I chuckled as I remembered back in the day doing 60 or so pushups, and being so proud of myself. That was before Master Yuen pointed out that some people do thousands of pushups in sets of a hundred. Ignominy was a powerful teacher for me.

The monster's head consisted of billionaire families that all had one thing in common, the promulgation and perpetuation of massive crimes against humanity. That was how all of them got to be so rich. According to our research at least.

In the case of the Rockefellers, a snake oil huckster and bigamist named William Avery Rockefeller taught his sons how to use deception to prey on the weak and the innocent in his pursuit of wealth and power. One of his sons, John D. Rockefeller, later took what his father had taught him, and destroyed the competition to his gasoline business. He did this by, under the ruse of Christian temperance, giving 4 million dollars to a group of old ladies and telling them to fight for Prohibition. They were successful in having the sale, production, importation, and transportation of alcoholic beverages banned. At the time, cars could run on gasoline or alcohol, and in some quarters, alcohol was the preferred fuel. Prohibition lasted for 13 years. During that period, the only fuel available to run cars was gasoline, John D.'s gasoline.

In 1938, John D. Rockefeller's Standard Oil of California joined with other companies to form National City Lines the express purpose of which was to buy local transit systems throughout the United States. They controlled transit systems in 45 cities. They used that control to convert the electric trolley lines to diesel bus lines giving them complete control of all surface travel in the country. It became known as the Great American Streetcar Scandal.

John D. next figured out that the internal combustion engine would not be able to consume all the oil he produced. So he had to create other outlets for its use. He began by buying a controlling interest in all the pharmaceutical companies that produced legal narcotics. Next, he donated huge sums to states in order for them to set up medical boards to issue licenses to practice medicine, and make it a crime to practice medicine without one. All other alternative medical practices were outlawed. He then gave those same states additional sums to establish medical schools in their land grant colleges with the condition that they teach exclusively pharmaceutical medicinal treatments. The final step was to generate a 'report' that established pharmaceutical medicinal treatments as superior to all others. John D. successfully gained control of the practice of medicine in the United States of America. Every hospital, every medical school, every doctor promoted pharmaceutical medicinal treatments as the end-all and be-all of health. And it all culminated in the use of 'medicines' manufactured from John D.'s oil.

John D. also said, "I would rather earn 1% off a 100

people's efforts than 100% off my own efforts." Again, the obvious question. How does it happen that these 100 people somehow leave 1% of their earnings just lying around for some John D. to stumble upon and earn? He used the word 'earn,' but in fact he meant steal. The man was a thief, and he and his extended family have been robbing all of us blind for generations.

After the curls, I did lateral raises. I pushed my arms out to the side and up over my head. I could feel the muscles in my shoulders begin to burn. I could feel myself involuntarily leaning back in order to get the weights up. Once I started, I remembered how much I hated them. I had to resist the temptation to throw my arms up, and then let them drop down. I could recall Master Yuen instructing me to control the weights, to not sling them. I tried to raise them up slowly. I could feel the sweat begin to bead on my brow. I did two sets of 25. I let my mind wander again to take it off the discomfort in my shoulders.

It was the Rockefeller family that invented chemotherapy using chemicals they supplied to the U.S. military during World War II. They then thwarted the development of various alternatives that would have competed with their cancer treatment, inventions like Dr. Royal Raymond Rife's Frequency Technology that cured 16 terminally ill cancer patients back in 1934. So Rife and his invention had to be discredited and destroyed.

They had also had other potentially viable cancer drug treatments discredited and banned by the FDA. These included Laetrile and Omniferon. In the case of Omniferon, they bankrupted the company, Viregen. It took them 25 years to do it, but they successfully thwarted the development of yet another potential cure for cancer.

In 1974, cannabis researchers at the Medical College of Virginia discovered that cannabis contains powerful cancer fighting properties. In 2000, researchers in Madrid, Spain, came to the same conclusion. However, the FDA, controlled by the Rockefellers, claimed that cannabis had no medicinal value.

As a result, millions of people have suffered and died. I wondered how the fuck the Rockefellers could sleep at night! That was why to kill a billionaire.

I became so annoyed with my musings that I lost count of my raises. I didn't want to start all over again, because I didn't want to put too much stress on any one muscle group. I wiped my brow with the back of my wrist. In so doing, I gathered swear into a little stream that ran directly into one of my eyes. It burned. My mouth was dry. I now fully understood why Master Yuen brewed tea before each workout session, lots of it. I was tempted to stop and go out for water. I decided that I needed to finish the raises first. So I did a few more to where I thought I might have ended had I not lost count. Then I went to the vending machine, and popped for an iced tea. It wasn't Master Yuen's green tea, but it would have to do.

John D. also bought, then supplied, the major food manufacturing and processing companies with the raw materials for their fertilizers and pesticides. In fact, it was the Rockefeller family through the Rockefeller Foundation that capitalized in America on the Green Revolution developed in Mexico. But they took it way past the humanitarian goal it was initially intended to serve. Family farms in America disappeared the way medical schools that didn't buy into the Rockefeller cancer scheme disappeared.

It was Henry Kissinger who in 1973 said, "He who controls the food supply controls the people." The Rockefellers, in collusion with the major food processing corporations, have taken steps to control the world's food supply. Those steps are: (1) genetically modify the food, (2) patent the GMOed seeds, and make it a crime to save seeds, then (3) force family farmers off their land. Once these steps are taken, the Rockefellers will control the world's food supply. They already own the entire medical chemical industry. Those same companies own all the companies that manufacture GMOed seeds as well as the companies that manufacture the pesticides to be sprayed on them. The final step is to eliminate totally the use of naturally occurring food seeds. At that point, all of humanity will be their slaves. And they get to do it legally thanks to an opinion authored in 2001 by the esteemed Mister Justice Clarence Uncle Thomas giving corporations the 'right' to patent seeds. Could this have been the *quid pro quo* for Ms. Thomas being involvement with the Tea Party and other groups funded by Koch cash, and the Justice himself getting huge fees for speaking engagements at Koch sponsored events?

After lateral raises, I did front raises. I pushed my arms out in front of me until they were shoulder high, then let them back down again. I remembered that I hated these, too. I found myself once again leaning back slightly for leverage in getting the weights up. I was beginning to tire. I needed to control my breathing. I inhaled through my nose and exhaled through my mouth with each raise. What the fuck made me think this was a good idea? I did another two sets of 25.

Were it not for billionaires, humanity would flourish.

Billionaires made their living by thwarting human progress for their own personal gain. Life was a game of give and take. But billionaires didn't play that game. For them, life was a game of take and take. They gave nothing, and they took everything.

Throughout modern history in America, and probably in the world, it was billionaires who had been the curse of democracy. In 1913, it was billionaires who established the Federal Reserve Bank. Since then, the American people have been paying trillions of dollars on loans made to the U.S. government. The income tax code was established that same year. And to cover their tracks, the Rockefellers formed their foundation that same year to dupe the public into believing their goals were merely philanthropic.

This was John D.'s dream come true. It was the major banks, through their investment banking functions that in the 2000s raped the stock market by performing naked short sales on small- and medium-sized companies, thus preventing the creation of millions of jobs over a span of fifteen years, and in the process, stealing the equity of all the shareholders in those companies. A handful of families have been draining American resources for over one hundred years. It was time for it to stop! It was time for the American people to get reparations! It was time to kill a billionaire!

After the front raises, I did some shoulder presses. I was so tired, I had to struggle to keep my balance. I felt myself wobble as I pushed the weights high over my head. I found myself staring up at the ceiling as I pushed. I let my gaze wander out the window at the snow and sleet being whipped by the wind. I kept my breathing steady, in through the nose, out through the mouth. I did two sets of 15.

Wasn't it John D. who said, "I don't want a nation of thinkers; I want a nation of workers?" The real question was, how does that statement square with the notion that this was a democracy where every person was in control of his own destiny? Apparently, John D. knew something that the rest of us didn't, and that something was that we didn't live in a democracy. His wealth was substantial enough that he could control our fates without us knowing that it was even being controlled.

More precisely, John D. said, "In our dreams, people yield themselves with perfect docility to our molding hands. The present education conventions of intellectual and character education fade from their minds, and, unhampered by tradition, we work our own good will upon a grateful and responsive folk. We shall not try to make these people, or any of their children, into philosophers, or men of science.

"We have not to raise up from them authors, educators, poets or men of letters. We shall not search for great artists, painters, musicians nor lawyers, doctors, preachers, politicians, statesmen – of whom we have an ample supply. The task is simple. We will organize children and teach them in a perfect way the things their fathers and mothers are doing in an imperfect way."

Who the fuck has such a twisted dream?! Only a Rockefeller! He admitted this madness in a speech in 1906 to the General Education Board which he himself founded in 1902. Initially, this was his plan for Black children in the southern states. In the end, it became his plan for all children. And this is the board that in 1960 became part of the Rockefeller Foundation.

I needed to do something easier. The curls and raises and shoulder presses had completely worn me out. I settled on shrugs. For these, I used 25 pound weights. I hunched my shoulders up and down, up and down. I could feel my shirt sticking to my back as I lifted my shoulders. I did three sets of 25.

Several of the people who were working out when I arrived were now either relaxing or gone. Only about half the original number of people were still present.

One young brother was sprawled out on his back on the bench press bench like a dead man, his muscular arms draped to the floor, knuckles on the rubber floor mat.

David Rockefeller followed closely in his granddaddy's footsteps. It was David Rockefeller who destroyed any chance that the United States of America had of retaining any form of democracy. It was David Rockefeller who formed the Trilateral Commission in 1973. The commission's task was to find out why there was so much unrest on college campuses in the 1960s. The commission published a report of its findings. The very title of the report was troubling. Its complete title was *The Crisis of Democracy: Report on the Governability of Democracies to the Trilateral Commission.*

Democracies are not governed; they themselves *do* the governing. So the very title of the report itself implied that someone wanted to control the democracy, that people could not be counted on to govern themselves. Or more exactly, the people would govern themselves in a way that was anathema to the interests of the very wealthy.

More specifically, Chapter III of the report outlined three areas where democracy in this country was flourishing: expanded education for the masses of people, the influence of national media on the power of the president, and the growing power of the Congress.

Little David saw each of these areas of progress as a problem, and each of these areas of progress has since been crushed.

I decided that was enough for the upper body. I needed to work on my legs. I walked around the room a couple of times to loosen my legs up. I did a few heel raises, maybe 20. Then I started with lunges using the 25 pound weights. They were too heavy, so I grabbed the 10 pounders. I didn't go down very low. My legs were already tired. I could hear the cartilage in my knees popping. I did the best I could. I did three sets of five on each leg.

First of all, Little David determined that Americans had too much education, that the expectations of women, Blacks and Latinos were too high. "People no longer felt the same compulsion to obey those whom they had previously considered superior to themselves in age, rank, status, expertise, character or talents." The report went on to say, "Authority based on hierarchy, expertise, and wealth all, obviously, ran counter to the democratic and egalitarian temper of the times, and during the 1960s, all three came under heavy attack."

So Little David's solution to that 'problem' was to limit access to education for the masses. Like his granddaddy, David didn't want a nation of thinkers. He wanted a nation of workers. So to make it hard for people to become thinkers, he, through his involvement with the Rockefeller Foundation, put into place policies that increased the cost of higher education, and reduced the availability of public education. His goal was to have corporations feed the people only as much as he wanted them to know. That was why to kill a billionaire.

After the lunges, I walked around the room a couple more times. I did a few more heel raises. I thought about doing some squats. I had wanted to do three sets of ten, but I fell over on the very first squat. I looked around to see who saw me fall, but I had the room to myself. The young brother who had been on the bench press bench was just leaving. I had so much trouble getting through the first set that I let that do it. Nothing like wobbly squats to make you change your mind about doing them.

With regard to the media, the report stated that "Truman had been able to govern the country with the cooperation of a relatively small number of Wall Street lawyers and bankers."

Remembering that statement now helped me regain my resolve. Democracies don't have one central ruler like a king. President Truman was supposed to be able to govern the country with the cooperation of Congress and the Judiciary. Wall Street lawyers and bankers were not supposed to be involved in the governing process at all. But given that some Rockefeller, and likely Little David himself, was one of those involved in that quote cooperation unquote, Little David felt obligated to promulgate the illusion that the president alone ran the country.

The report went on to say that "There is . . . considerable evidence to suggest that the development of television journalism contributed to the undermining of governmental authority." What the report failed to point out was that government derived its authority from the people. Little David Rockefeller would have us believe that it was the other way around, that the people derive their rights from the government. He would have us believe that the exercise of our constitutionally guaranteed First Amendment right to a free and vibrant press contributed to the undermining of governmental authority, when in fact, the press kept the people apprised of whether or not the government was doing the people's bidding.

I had enough of strength training. I walked around the room a couple more times to catch my breath. The rubber mat on the floor yielded ever so slightly under each step.

Then I started in on technique practice. I needed to work on my kicks by shadow boxing. Low kicks came first, kicks with the ball of the foot to the ankles and knees. I did combinations of two and three kicks alternating one leg, then the other. I wanted to do sets, but working the combinations until I got them perfect seemed to flow better, so I went with that. I switched to kicks with the blade of the foot. Then I switched to kicks that alternated the blade with the ball of the foot. I did a few kicks with the heel of the foot, all low to the toe, arch, ankle, shin, knee areas. My breathing as I kicked was smooth or forceful as needed, but always controlled.

The report further said that "it is a long-established and familiar political fact that within a city or even within a state, the power of local press serves as a major check on the power of local government. . . . Only in recent years, however, has there come into existence a national press with the economic independence and communications reach to play a role with respect to the president that a local newspaper plays with respect to a mayor. This marks the emergence of a very significant check on presidential power."

This was, in fact, the way a democracy was supposed to work. The president is *not* supposed to have unchecked power.   David Rockefeller, however, took issue. He had his friend, Rupert Murdoch, begin buying media outlets.   Rupert bought his first American newspaper in 1973, the same year Little David formed the Trilateral Commission.   Rupert founded the Fox Broadcasting Company in 1986.   Because of Rupert Murdoch, the mainstream press in America today is a joke.   We have devolved from Chet Huntley, David Brinkley and Walter Cronkite down to Bill O'Reilly. No hard news, only infotainment and polemic disguised as news.   Rupert   Murdoch   used   Edward   Bernays's techniques for manipulating public thought, telling people what to think, what opinions to hold, rather than providing information that allowed people to derive their own opinions.   Bernays felt this manipulation of social thought was necessary because independent thought in society was irrational and dangerous, and had to be controlled.   Certainly mainstream media today provides nothing that would allow the citizenry to question the actions of anyone in authority, let alone the president.

On July 31, 1970, in his farewell broadcast, Chet Huntley characterized American journalism as the best in the world. Rupert Murdoch fixed that. The press that served us so well in the 1960s and early 1970s was gone. That was why to kill a billionaire.

Kicks to the ankles and knees seemed to flow right into kicks to the groin, front kicks and side kicks. I worked them with the front leg and the back leg. Then I changed my stance so that the other leg was now the front leg, and worked them all again. My breathing felt good, and my balance was coming back. I did a couple of back kicks. Then I got all the way down on the mat for my back kicks. That was a mistake. My arms were so tired, I had trouble getting back up. I finished the tea I had gotten earlier, and rested for a few minutes.

With regard to Congress, the report said that "the 1960s and early 1970s also saw a reassertion of the power of Congress. . . . These years saw the emergence, first in the Senate then in the House, of a new generation of congressional activists willing to challenge established authority in their own chambers as well as in the presidency." Again, democracy was working the way it was supposed to work. And again, Little David took exception. This time, he called on the Koch brothers, David and Charles. Together, they financed the forming of the Tea Party. These days, thanks to Tea Party loyalists, Congress does little if anything meaningful. They spend all their time bickering or doing the bidding of the billionaires who financed them. Their stated agenda is to shut the government down. No more of those pesky "congressional activists willing to challenge established authority in their own chambers as well as in the presidency." Their goal is the destruction of democracy in America, because that was David Rockefeller's goal.

All progress in American society has since been crushed like a rice puff under a flat iron skillet, and David Rockefeller is the one who crushed it. *That* was why to kill a billionaire, and Little David was the perfect candidate.

XX

Retribution. Grandma Daughter used to talk about it all the time. She would say, "The wheels of justice grind slowly, but they grind exceedingly fine." Was it she who told me that it was from a long forgotten poet in Africa? I couldn't remember. But the image of a large stone grinding wheel rolling over the naked bodies of evil-doers and crunching them like corn flakes has flooded my mind countless times.

Retribution. Recompense. Punishment. These were the words she used when she talked about my father before she killed him. She even warned him once, during one of his Friday night tirades when he would come home drunk and beat Mama and her for not having dinner on the table ready. Never mind it was midnight when he finally got home. She told him that he was going to pay for the pain he was meting out. He blackened her eye, and that was the only warning she gave him. His warning was more powerful than hers.

Outside his hearing, she quoted Deuteronomy, 'Vengeance is Mine, and retribution, In due time their foot will slip; For the day of their calamity is near, And the impending things are hastening upon them.'

She believed it, and she acted on it. Soon thereafter,

my father was dead.

The problem with retribution was that sometimes it came too slowly. And retribution in the hereafter was no retribution at all. Grandma Daughter wanted to see retribution in her own time, with her own eyes. And she did.

It troubled me that I had become so much like my father. The realization was slow in coming, but it was unmistakable. I could not help recollecting Grandma Daughter's admonition in Deuteronomy. I could not help feeling the anger rise up in me when faced with inequities. That was part of the reason I was in the business I was in. Assassins got to exact retribution. We got to make it right. To that extent, I knew I was just like her.

It seemed odd that my father's flaw was in me, and Grandma Daughter's flaw was in me as well. He had a love of inflicting pain. That love got him killed, because he inflicted pain on the wrong people. He inflicted pain more than once on Grandma Daughter. She had the need to exact retribution. That need led her to kill him. Those flaws were both in me.

I wondered if the notion of retribution played any part in members of *Seine Kinder* so hoping the prophet had returned. Was that my mission? Was that what I was here to do? It seemed like such a daunting task to exact retribution on behalf of humanity. Individual retribution was hard enough. I could scarcely imagine what retribution by a prophet even meant.

Retribution and restitution. They went hand in hand. In my business, restitution was implied in retribution. Retribution *was* the payback. For some of my clients, restitution came after the fact in the form of goods that could now be reclaimed, or payments that could now be recouped.

The 23rd Psalm in the Holy Bible embodied the concept of restitution. Grandma Daughter read it often.

The Lord is my Shepherd; I shall not want.

He maketh me to lie down in green pastures:

He leadeth me beside the still waters.

He restoreth my soul:

He leadeth me in the paths of righteousness for His name's sake.

Yea, though I walk through the valley of the shadow of death,

I will fear no evil: For thou art with me;

Thy rod and thy staff, they comfort me.

Thou preparest a table before me in the presence of mine enemies;

Thou annointest my head with oil; My cup runneth over.

Surely goodness and mercy shall follow me all the days of my life,

and I will dwell in the House of the Lord forever.

'I shall not want' meant exactly that. I shall not want! 'He restoreth my soul' meant I have been made whole again. That was what restitution was! 'Thou preparest a table before me in the presence of mine enemies.' Take that, punk! 'My cup runneth over.'

It was time for somebody to get retribution, and for humanity to get restitution. Not in the hereafter. Rather, in the here and now. Maybe that's what my Great Uncle Buddy had really been about all along. And maybe that's what his followers expected of me as the heir apparent. I felt humbled, and, at the same time, I felt apprehensive. I wanted to make the right choices, and be worthy of that expectation. I wanted to make it count.

XXI

Almost instinctively, I shot off a spinning reverse roundhouse. It surprised me, because I had not intended to do any exotic kicks in this workout. I had wanted to stick to the basics. Spinning kicks were never easy, because they required excellent balance and concentration. If not done right, they could lead to damaged knees or loss of equilibrium resulting in an uncontrollable fall and serious injury. Especially for those who had not done their Iron Body exercises. Master Yuen taught that exotic kicks were too flashy to be of any serious value anyway. But my body felt it, and did it. And it was perfect. I didn't think about it. I just did it. Then I faked a spinning reverse roundhouse, and followed it with a roundhouse with the other leg. I was on a roll.

There is a technique in the Chinese martial arts called trapping hands. The object is to momentarily render the opponents hands useless, and in that moment, attack a vital spot. The same holds true for fighting the monster. The monster's minions, its armies and law enforcement agencies, are its talons. There is no point to thwarting the talons unless that thwarting exposes an opening to strike at the monster's head. Better to avoid the talons altogether.   Like a boxer slipping a punch, slip the talons, and swing for the head. Always swing for the head. Always kill a billionaire.

Again, without thinking about it, I lapsed into hand techniques as I kicked. Inside circles, outside circles, Wing Chung punches and blocks. My arms were tired, but they seemed to move of their own volition. Shadow boxing was an art in itself. And without meaning to be, I was in a shadow boxing dance. It was as if my tiredness were irrelevant. I didn't think about it. I just danced.

Sometimes, the monster's talons *do* need to be severed.   Sometimes, a cop needs to be killed. Christopher Dorner knew that. He said as much in his manifesto. "The enemy combatants in LA are not the citizens and suspects, it's the police officers." And not just in LA. Flint Farmer was shot three times in the back as he lay face down on the ground by Chicago Police Officer Gildardo Sierra in Chicago.   Eric Garner was strangled to death by New York City Police Officer Daniel Pantaleo in Staten Island. Michael Brown was shot in the face then in the top of his head as he stood with his hands in the air by Ferguson Police Officer Darren Wilson in Ferguson, Missouri. Antonio Zambrano-Montes was shot and killed by Ryan Flanagan, Adam Wright and

Adrian Alaniz in Pasco, Washington. Sometimes, you need to pop a cop. Even if it is just to make yourself feel better. Sometimes, it just feels good to kill a racist. But I had to be careful not to delude myself into believing that killing a cop would in any way thwart the monster. Quoting Dorner again, "I am here to change and make policy. The culture of LAPD versus the community and honest/good officers needs to and will change. I am here to correct and calibrate your moral compasses to true north." I might from time to time need to re-calibrate a cop's moral compass, but the killing of cops should not, if possible, be an end in itself, just as trapping hands is never an end in itself.

My body was really flowing now. My kicks were high and fast, then low and tight. I did a few Muay Thai elbow strikes. I did fakes and weaves followed by Tai Chi moves that I wasn't sure I even remembered. Remembered or not, there they were. The dance changed in character from one moment to the next, from one movement to the next.

In retrospect, that was the mistake Ida and I had made years ago. We struck at a police station. Ismaaiyl Brinsley made the same mistake when he shot officers Liu and Ramos. We blunted a couple of the monster's talons. But we did nothing to stop the monster. The monster simply grew new talons. In Brinsley's case, the real targets, parts of the monster's head, were right across the East River on Park Avenue in Manhatten. That's where he should have struck.

There was also no point in attacking government offices. One of the functions of the government is to take the blame for the atrocities committed by the rich. Don't get mad at the government; get mad at the rich. They run the government. Anyone running for the lofty office of President of the United States of America must go begging for campaign money to the rich. If he does not do what they tell him to do, he will not be president. And because the super rich have indirect control of the Secret Team, an elite section of the CIA that operates outside the normal bounds set for the agency, indeed outside the bounds of the law, and which conducts covert operations worldwide during peacetime and war, if the president they supported gets out of line, they will simply have him killed. That is what happened to President John F. Kennedy. He broke ranks with the people who financed him, and they killed him for it. They stole his splattered brain, and put it in Geronimo's skull.

David Rockefeller was friends with Allen Dulles, Richard Helms, Archibald Bulloch Roosevelt, Jr., and William Bundy. All these men were either CIA directors or career CIA officers. Roosevelt retired from the CIA in 1974, and took a position at J.P. Morgan-Chase where he was closely associated with David Rockefeller.

Bundy was a member of the Council on Foreign Relations from 1972 to 1984, and was offered by the Council's chairman, David Rockefeller, to be the Council's president. Bundy was also Honorary American Secretary General of the Bilderberg Meetings from 1975 to 1980. David Rockefeller is the only member of the Advisory Board for the Bilderberg Group.

Finally, on November 28, 1961, President Kennedy presented Dulles with the National Security Medal at the CIA Headquarters in Langley, Virginia. The next day, November 29, the White House released a resignation letter signed by Dulles. Two years to the day later, President Lyndon Baines Johnson appointed Dulles as one of seven commissioners of the Warren Commission to investigate the assassination of President Kennedy. Dulles must have been supremely satisfied to be in a position of cover-up the real details of Kennedy's murder.

I remembered a conversation I had had on that topic with Menachem.

"If you recall," he had said, "it was the CIA's Secret Team that orchestrated Kennedy's death."

"Wait," I said, "the CIA orchestrated Kennedy's death?"

"You didn't know that?" he asked back.

"You can only know something that is a fact," I said. "And it has not been established that the CIA having killed Kennedy is a fact."

Menachem remained silent. He had that little supercilious grin on his face that I had seen when I was in Israel and he had said something that he thought I should have known but didn't.

Then he let me off the hook.

"Maybe that is information I had access to because I was in Mossad," he said.

David Rockefeller had ample opportunity to contribute to the planning of that assassination and its cover-up. I remembered my roommates in Tel Aviv telling me about the CIA assassinations of Malcolm X and Patrice Lumumba. I wondered if Little David could have been involved in the Congo Crisis and the murder of Prime Minister Lumumba.

The Rockefellers had similar influence in the FBI. After the 1919 Anarchist Bombings where John D. was one of the targets, then-U.S. Attorney General A. Mitchell Palmer formed a new intelligence division of the Justice Department. He appointed J. Edgar Hoover to head it up. Hoover oversaw the infamous Palmer Raids, wherein by 1920, he had amassed a list of over 60,000 political radicals, arrested over 10,000, and deported nearly 600 people. In 1924, the intelligence division of the Justice Department became the Federal Bureau of Investigation, and Hoover became the director.

It was during this time that Marcus Garvey formed the Universal Negro Improvement Association. Garvey's plan was for Black people to be a completely independent and international power base. A coordinated European and North American attack on his plan killed it.

By 1935, John, Jr. and J. Edgar were photographed together with John, Jr. being fingerprinted as part of a program to fingerprint everyone in the country. Clearly, the idea of controlling the masses wasn't new.

The FBI was conceived with the expressed mission of crushing political descent of any kind. It crushed the labor movement in the 20s; it crushed the communists in the 20s; it crushed Garvey in the 20s. It crushed the Black Panthers in the 60s and 70s. In crushed the American Indian Movement. It crushed the Free Puerto Rico movement. It is crushing Muslims today. And all at the behest of the billionaire cabal.

The super rich think nothing about putting innocent people in prison for the rest of their lives or of killing people. Any plan to kill *them* would simply be leveling the playing field. So I knew not to bother assassinating a president or any other political figure. Instead, our plan was to assassinate the billionaire who financed the political figure's campaign. That was why to kill a billionaire.

I felt myself slowing down. I settled into a Tai Chi routine that I hadn't done in years. It didn't matter that I couldn't remember the original sequence. I created my own sequence, and kept going. My body seemed to want to go as slowly as it could. I imagined light coming from my fingertips and palms, light that had the power to kill. I felt invincible.

The main reason to kill a billionaire is that it is the only recourse. For them, the power of love will never overcome the love of power, and the government is powerless against them. Everything that is wrong with society as we know it can be traced back to some billionaire or billionaire family. Irreversible damage to the environment? The Gulf oil spill where 3.19 million barrels of oil poured into the Gulf of Mexico in 2010? A billionaire did it. Plastic bottles and nets and ropes and bags clogging the oceans and killing them? A billionaire did it. Militarization of the local police making tanks and military grade firearms available to be deployed to control peaceful protests? A billionaire did it. Stagnated growth of the middle class where since 1980, the average income for the middle class has increased about 20 percent, but the income for the super rich has increased by over 280 percent? A billionaire did it. Failure to repair the infrastructure where bridges and roads across the country are crumbling? A billionaire did it. The war on terror? The surveillance state? Perpetual war? The overthrow of democracies in Latin America, especially in Brazil where then-President Goulart had proposed basic reforms that benefitted the poor and Afro-Brazilians? A billionaire did it. Assassinate democratically elected Chilean President Salvador Allende to install Augusto Pinochet who then brought in the Chicago Boys, educated in the main at Rockefeller's University of Chicago school of economics, to fuck up the economy? A billionaire did it. Contract the money supply in order to generate foreclosures where working families are losing their homes and Wall Street bankers are getting bailed out? A billionaire did it. Everything that is fucked up about the world is the result of billionaire greed. Everything!

And their plan for humanity in the future is even more dire. First of all, they want to cull about 90% of us. Then they want to implant microchips in the rest of us. This according to Nicholas Rockefeller himself. These chips will have everything about us on it, including our bank accounts. That way, if we don't follow their orders, they'll simply turn off the chip leaving us with nothing. That was why to kill a billionaire.

Right in the middle of my Tai Chi routine, I lapsed into a drunken mode. I had never done this before, but it felt right. I repeated some of the sequences I had already done, but now I did them as a drunk. I could feel myself bobbing and weaving in an unpredictable manner. I could feel myself spontaneously creating moves, then firing off strikes and kicks from within them. Even I couldn't be sure what I would do next. It was all up to the spirit that moved through me.

Billionaires have bought so many state and federal legislators and officers through fixed and stolen elections and high-priced lobbyists, that the laws being passed do not apply to them. In fact, they see to it that laws are passed that benefit only them. And because they have had their presidential flunkies pack the U.S. Supreme Court with their judicial flunkies, some of whom are themselves millionaires thanks to speaking engagements financed by the Koch brothers, we get bullshit decisions like Citizens United that grant the billionaire cabal the 'right' to fuck the people even more. Therefore, there are no organized structures in place that can remove them from power. Even the United Nations was built on Rockefeller land. It follows that if the people ever expect to regain their freedom, they will have to take matters into their own hands.

Death was the only option. And not just death, it must be death on a large scale. Again, Maximilien Robespierre was right. Common people in every country of the world must rise up and kill the super rich. Billionaires must be killed, because that is the only way to bring them to justice. They are the hidden hand. All of them have committed, or have benefitted from their forefathers having committed, crimes against humanity, be it slavery, the federal reserve bank, gutting the stock market, or suppressing thousands of inventions that would have benefitted mankind. And they don't care what we think. Polls may show that Americans are sick of war, but billionaires will send us off to die anyway. We protest. We picket. We petition. But it is all for nothing. They don't listen. They don't care. Everything they do is for the benefit of themselves, and never for the benefit of the people. They see us as their cattle. You wouldn't hesitate to kill a cow if you wanted a T-bone steak, would you? All the lowing in the world would not matter. That is how they see us. Their answer to "No Blood for Oil" is "Your Blood for My Oil." To "War is NOT the Answer" they reply that "War is the ONLY Answer." "No War No Way" becomes "Yes War Always." "Green Jobs Now" becomes

"No Jobs Now." "Books Not Bombs" becomes "Bombs Not Books." "Smash Racism" becomes "Racism as a Tool." "Stop Drone Attacks" becomes "More Drone Attacks." When we take to the streets, they send the police to quash and arrest us. The only thing a billionaire will understand is death. Let them taste what we have been tasting for generations. In an interview with Ben Fulford in Tokyo, Japan, on November 14, 2007, Little David admitted that he was proud of what his family had done. William Avery Rockefeller's apple certainly did not fall very far from the tree. *That* was why to *kill* a billionaire.

I wound up the Tai Chi routine and took a deep breath. I exhaled slowly. I could feel it. I could feel that my mood had changed. I felt tired, but satisfied. I took a quick shower, and headed back to the house. The dark clouds were still swirling, but it didn't bother me as much. I needed to get to work planning my next move. The sleet pelting me in the face actually felt good. My resolve was back.

On the drive home, I realized that I had not thought about *Das Innerste Feuer* for over an hour and a half. But wait! They were the ones who should be afraid. I was the one who was in the business of killing people for a living! All I had to do was find them.

I needed to go back to Rainbow Beach. I was already

on Lake Shore Drive heading north, so I took the Foster exit, cut under the bridge, and turned left onto the southbound ramp. Resolve is a motherfucker! I knew what I had to do.

The sleet was turning into heavy snow, so I couldn't really get up any speed driving there, but before long, I was turning left at 79th Street into Rainbow Park. I wound around past the entrance to the water filtration plant, past the new field house, to the far end of the parking lot. Because it was winter, I had expected mine to be the only car there. It wasn't.

The other car, a late model silver VW, was parked on the east side of the lot, facing the lake. Not wanting to be too close to it, I parked on the west side of the lot, also facing the lake. I backed my car into the parking space until it bounced against the concrete marker.

I had come here thinking I would walk over to the tree where I had been sitting the day I got shot. But I changed my mind. The snow was too heavy. The wind was blowing too hard. It was too cold. So I sat staring out over the water through the white cloud of swirling snow and sleet.

After a few minutes, the driver's side door of the VW opened about a foot. It was as if the person inside was contemplating getting out, but was having second thoughts for the same reasons I had had second thoughts. Then the door slammed shut.

All at once, the door opened again, this time all the way. A child dangled his legs out the door, then slid from the car seat to the ground. That's when I noticed it wasn't a child at all. It was a dwarf. I chuckled aloud at the irony. The last time I was here, I saw a dwarf. Now, on my first time back since then, I saw a dwarf again.

I couldn't put my finger on it, but there was something familiar about him. He pulled his collar up against the wind, then braced himself for I didn't know what. He tried running a couple of steps, but realized there was no point. The wind was too high and the snow was too deep. His running those few steps, however, was enough. I knew who he was. He was my dwarf, the one who shot me, then ran off decades ago, leaving me to die.

My first thought was to kill him, to get revenge. But could I be sure? This snow was heavy. And my view across the lot was not clear. Maybe I was being paranoid because of my recent contacts with *Das Innerste Feuer*. I watched as the dark figure that I thought might be him trudge through the snow in the direction of my tree. Before long, he was completely out of sight, obscured by the blowing snow.

I don't know what it was about seeing him disappear

like that, but I was suddenly reminded of my escape from Mighty Red's house back in Germany. I had heard someone, a man, calling her name, Anna, aloud, and rummaging around in the kitchen down stairs, and I had taken that moment to leave. It was from there that I had bolted to Spain.

The dwarf was gone from view long enough that the snow began to build up on my windshield wiper blades. They swept two streaked arcs across my window. A thin glaze of ice began to form that the wipers could not remove. I got out of the car. I eased around my open door to where I could wipe the glass with my open hand. I tried to knock the ice from the wiper blades while they were still going. Having gotten some of the ice off of one blade, I decided to try my luck with the other one. I eased around the front of the car to the passenger side. Just as I had gotten about half the ice off that blade, someone tapped my elbow. I looked around. It was him.

"Excuse me, . . . ," he stopped when he recognized me. He had been about to give me a scrapper to help remove the snow from my windshield. The bastard was being a good Samaritan!

I recognized his voice from the last time I saw him. I remembered him asking, "Are you the one?" I also recognized his eyes. They were such a dark brown, they looked almost black. They had crow's feet now, deep and long. The last time I looked into those eyes, he was brandishing a gun. Seconds later, I was slumped on the ground bleeding.

Apparently, he was having a similar recollection as *he* looked into *my* eyes. He stepped back and dropped the scrapper. He reached for his pocket. I stepped towards him and bent down and grabbed his arm. He was only about four feet tall. His arms were short, but very powerful. He executed a perfect little Grey Cloud to break my grip, then stepped around and threw a solid punch to the side of my thigh right at that acupuncture point midway between the hip and the knee. This little bastard was well-trained! I had the advantage of surprise, though. He had no way of knowing that I, too, was well-trained. I faked being stunned, and leaned over as if favoring that leg. He dropped his guard and reached again for his pocket. Right at that instant, I threw a front kick with the leg he thought was injured. Because I had just worked out, it too was perfect. It had form. It had power. It had chi. I caught him right under his chin with the ball of my foot. There was a cracking sound when my foot made contact, and his head snapped back hard. I didn't know if it was his jaw or his neck that broke. I really didn't care. The kick was so hard, it lifted him completely off the ground. He landed on the snow-covered concrete like a rock, out cold, maybe dead. I didn't bother to check.

I emptied his pockets. The pocket he had been trying to reach had a box cutter. I threw his things onto the passenger seat of my car, then drove it across the lot to his car. I could feel the wheels slipping as they tried to get traction. I took everything out of his car after marveling over the special devices he had installed to allow him to drive, a booster for the seat, and blocks for the peddles. I slashed all the tires. I removed the license plates. These were new, and might be useful on a future job. By the time I was done, he was covered with enough snow that he looked like a little white grave. I drove gingerly along the road out of the park, and headed north on South Shore Drive.

Traffic was so slow and visibility so poor, it took nearly two hours to get home. The crosswind off the lake was hard and cold and a solid sheet of white snow. It rocked the car making the car hard to control, even at low speeds. The defoggers barely cleared the windshield. I could not help pondering the notion of moving to a warmer, drier state.

XXII

Once upstairs, as I sat wallowing in my newfound self-confidence, my muscles beginning to tighten up and ache, Menachem's phone rang again.

"Forget the Rockefellers," he said. "We should go after one of the Rothschilds."

"What?"

"Forget the Rockefellers."

"I heard what you said."

"We need to get a Rothschild. Jacob, maybe Evelyn. Maybe even Jacob's daughter, Hannah."

"I heard that part, too."

"So what is the problem?"

"What difference does it make," I asked, "which one we kill first?"

"The Rothschilds are much worse than the Rockefellers."

"Not possible," I said.

"To begin with," he said, "the Rothschilds have been at it way longer, three hundred years. The Rockefellers have been at it for only about a century."

"Time in grade doesn't count in this profession," I answered. "What have they done?"

"You mean besides finance the transatlantic slave trade

of Africans for over a hundred years?"

I couldn't believe this bastard was playing the race card. He knew that would pique my interest. And it did. But I stayed calm.

"Yes," I answered, "besides the European slave trade."

"The Rothschilds are trillionaires," he said. "They have created the worlds billionaires, including the Rockefellers."

"Besides that?" I asked.

"At the insistence of a Rothschild, the British attacked America to start the War of 1812. Does that count?"

"It counts," I said.

"But specific instances of crimes against humanity are harder to pinpoint with the Rothschilds," he continued. "Because their wealth is so vast, they manipulate countries. Their starting the War of 1812 is only one example."

"I guess you have others?"

"Yes, of course," he answered. "In 1914, the Rothschild banks in Germany, Britain and France loaned money to those governments in order for them each to finance their respective war efforts. The Rothschild media companies in those countries, Wolff in Germany, Reuters in England, and Havas in France, then fomented war."

"Clever," I said.

"I know, right?" he replied. "The Rothschilds didn't care who won the war. They got richer no matter who won, because part of the contract for the loans to each of them was that the victor would pay the debt of the loser."

"Such a deal!"

"Such a deal indeed. And it gets better," he continued. "The Rothschilds made a deal with Britain to bring the United States into that war and for Britain giving the Rothschilds Palestine in return."

"What?!"

"You heard me right. Britain was losing the war. They needed help."

"So we got dragged into that war because of the Rothschilds?" I was stunned.

"Exactly," he answered. "Yankee Doodle went to war so that the Rothschilds could get Palestine."

"So present-day Israel is really Rothschildland."

"Yes. It took another 35 or so years for Britain to deliver, but deliver they did."

I had to think for a minute. It sounded like Menachem was right. The Rothschilds *were* a much greater enemy of humanity than the Rockefellers. That's when I thought about Nelson Rockefeller and the shit he pulled. I kept it to myself, though.

"What about simply nationalizing all the banks?" I asked.

"That would take years, and would have to be a worldwide effort with no guarantee of success."

"Mass killings are no guarantee of success either," I countered.

"No, but this way we have direct control over what we decide to do. Nationalizing banks requires legislatures and proposed laws and politics. I don't know about you, but I'm no politician."

"There is one point that I do not understand," I said. "How did the Rothschilds get all these people to do their bidding?"

"They threatened them and their entire families with death. Every man, woman and child."

"Politicians?" I asked. "Senators? The president?!"

"Absolutely!" he answered. "Two United States presidents have already been assassinated for the exact same reason. Who do you suppose they were?"

"I only know of two," I answered, "Lincoln and Kennedy."

"And why do you suppose they were killed?"

"You've told me about Kennedy. But about Lincoln, I have no clue. In fact, does anybody know?"

"Oh, yes," he answered. "Everybody on the inside

knows."

"Okay," I said. "What's the reason?"

"They were both killed because they each tried to make the United States of America financially independent."

"What does that mean?" I asked.

"In 1861, President Lincoln needed money to finance the civil war. The Rothschild banks, the only banks that had on hand the sums he needed, offered loans at around 25% interest, maybe more. Lincoln decided to print his own U.S. currency rather than pay that kind of interest. He was assassinated in 1865."

"So what's the connection?" I asked.

"Lincoln made it clear to congress earlier in 1865 that the Rothschild banks were his greatest enemies, greater even than the Southern Army."

"That's pretty thin," I said. "Do you have any more on Kennedy?"

"Same thing," he said. "On June 4th, 1963, President Kennedy signed an executive order that returned to the United States government the power to issue its own money. On November 22nd of that same year, Kennedy was shot and killed. Johnson was no fool. He knew who killed Kennedy and why. He rescinded that order the same day on the flight from Dallas to Washington."

"That's a little more convincing," I said.

"You know the irony?" he asked. "Justice Powell tried to warn Kennedy that even the president might not be able to control the CIA and the Department of Defense, which was heavily infiltrated by the CIA."

"I didn't know that," I said.

"Well, did you know about Teddy Roosevelt?" he asked.

"No, what about him?"

"In 1902, J.P. Morgan of J.P. Morgan and Company fame, you know, the House of Morgan, . . ."

"Yes," I interrupted, "I know J.P. Morgan."

"Okay," he continued, "Morgan met with Teddy Roosevelt in order to keep Teddy from busting up a railroad monopoly Morgan owned. It didn't work. Teddy busted him up. Mind you, this is the same J.P. Morgan who thwarted Tesla's plan to provide humanity with unlimited free electric power. Remember that?"

I didn't. My remembrance, and I didn't recall how I knew it, was that Tesla had been working on the wireless transmission of electrical power. Or maybe he had been working on a coil to use electric power more efficiently. I wasn't sure. It didn't matter. The plans for both these innovations were destroyed in a fire in his studio on March 13, 1895, set by, some say, J.P. Morgan's goons.

"Well, later," Menachem continued, "in 1907, during the banking crisis that he himself created, Morgan concocted the scheme to monopolize banking. But he had to wait until Teddy was out of office, because he knew Teddy would bust that up, too. Teddy's term ended in 1909. In 1910, Morgan invited Senator Nelson Aldrich and a group of bankers that included Paul Warburg to Jekyll Island to draft the law that would create the Federal Reserve Bank."

"*The* Paul Warburg?" I asked. I thought I remembered the name from a flyer I had seen when I was stationed in Germany years ago. At that time, he was one of the richest men in Germany. Or maybe it was his family. That's when I remembered that Nelson Rockefeller's middle name was Aldrich. He was named after that motherfucker!

"That's right," Menachem answered. "Warburg was a representative of the Rothschild banking dynasty, and the chief architect of the proposed new law. But to their chagrin, Teddy decided to run for president again in 1912. Believing their plan would be thwarted, the big banks hired Schrank to kill Teddy. Teddy survived the attack, but he lost that election anyway to Wilson. The next year, the very first year of Wilson's presidency, Aldrich introduced the bill he had helped draft at Jekyll Island. Teddy never would have signed that law. But Wilson did, because he knew what they had just tried to do to Teddy. And here is another little tidbit," he offered. "After all that campaign talk about change and reforming Wall Street, Obama, after he got elected, nominated Ben Bernanke to head the Federal Reserve Board for another four years. Do you remember that?"

"Yes, I remember." I did remember, but I was still back at John, Jr. naming one of his sons after this asshole Aldrich. On the other hand, John, Jr.'s wife was the asshole's daughter. Maybe they were merely naming him after his grandfather, and not commemorating what the grandfather had done.

"This is the same Federal Reserve Board for which the bankers tried to kill Teddy."

"Yes," I said, "I see the connection."

"But did you see the footage?"

"What footage?"

"The footage of Obama making that nomination."

"I must have missed that."

"No matter," he said. "You might have missed what I am talking about even if you saw the footage."

"Missed what?"

"The grimace."

"What grimace?"

"Obama's grimace."

"Obama grimaced?"

"Yes," he answered, "he did."

"But, why?"

"That is the magic question, isn't it? And the answer is because he did not want to nominate Bernanke to that post again. He wanted to make good on his campaign promise of change."

"Then why did he do it?"

"Because Rothchilds' goon, David Rockefeller, gave him the message."

"Which was?"

"Nominate Bernanke or die. He reminded Obama that he, David, ran the CIA, and that the CIA blew Kennedy's brains out on his order. He warned Obama that if he didn't nominate Bernanke, he would blow his brains out, too."

"So he punked out," I said.

"Yes," he confirmed, "he punked out. And more than that," Menachem continued, "after all that talk about reforming Wall Street, Obama make Tim Geithner, who had been president of the Federal Reserve Bank of New York, Secretary of the Treasury. He made Gary Gensler, who had worked at Goldman Sachs for 18 years, chairman of the Commodity Futures Trading Commission, and he made Larry Summers, who had received millions in speaking fees from Goldman Sachs and JPMorgan Chase among others, director of the National Economic Council."

"The dude must have been scared," I said.

"Hell, yeah, he was scared," Menachem said. "And not just him."

"There were others?" I asked.

"*Yes*, there were others," he said. "Every president since Kennedy has been reminded of Kennedy's fate. Johnson was so scared, he declined to run for a second term. Nixon publicly lamented the weight of the nightmare any president endures because of the Deep State that is David Rockefeller and the CIA and the Department of Defense. And Obama also scared Eric Holder, and made him punk out. I know you remember the Holder quote 'too big to jail,' don't you?"

"Yeah, I remember."

"Well, what the fuck do you think that meant?"

"That the litigation would cost too much," I answered.

"Hell, no, that's not what it meant!"

His reaction took me aback. That meaning was so obvious, I could not imagine what else it could possibly be.

"It meant," he continued, "that there is a class of people for whom the laws of this country do not apply! And Holder's public announcement to the serfs and slaves meant don't even bother to try. *That* is what it meant!"

There was a taste in my mouth like bile. I didn't want to swallow, and I couldn't spit it out.

"So what you're saying is that nobody in government can loosen the stranglehold these bastards have on the American economy."

"Not just the American economy," he corrected, "the world economy."

"I guess that means it is up to us."

"Yes," he confirmed, "it is up to us."

I thought for a moment, then asked, "But what about the shit Nelson pulled?"

"What shit?" he asked back.

"What shit indeed," I answered. "Nelson Rockefeller served as the 49th Governor of New York from 1959 to 1973. During his term, he shepherded into existence the Depository Trust Company which now owns all the stock in all the companies in America. Nobody in this country owns stocks anymore. The Rockefellers own it all."

"I had heard that," he said.

"The Rockefellers formed the DTC ostensibly to facilitate the transfer of stock certificates," I continued. "But in order to be a part of that system, companies were required to transfer ownership of their stock to the DTC.

The ex-owners were now beneficiaries in some twisted way of the right that ownership conferred. However, if the Rockefellers decided to simply keep the stock, that would be that.

"This is the exact same ploy that his granddaddy used in 1871 when he formed the South Improvement Company. The snake oil huckster would have been proud. Back then, once the unsuspecting businessmen joined up with that company, they soon realized that according to the fine print they had given up all control and ownership of their companies to John D. Senior. The same thing has happened here. The Rockefellers own all the stock that is traded through the DTC."

"I had *not* heard that," he corrected.

"Well, had you heard this? As governor, Nelson Rockefeller created the Narcotic Addiction and Control Commission in 1967, ostensibly aimed at helping addicts get clean. This was during the time when he was making nice with Dr. King, acting as if his motives were purely philanthropic, donating money to bail out jailed freedom riders, and all. And after King got shot, he flew to Atlanta for the funeral. But to show you how much of a snake the man was, at the start of the new legislative session in January 1973, he introduced a new and aggressive anti-drug law to the residents of New York State. Its aim was 'to make the selling or conspiracy to sell hard drugs, the possession or conspiracy to possess large quantities of narcotics and the commission of violent crimes by persons who had ingested hard drugs punishable by the mandatory sentence of life imprisonment.'"

"A life sentence for possession? That's harsh!"

"Harsh indeed. And it was aimed at Black folks," I said. "This meant, in practice, that anyone convicted of selling or possessing any quantity of any 'narcotic' drug, including marijuana, hallucinogens, amphetamines or depressants, would, if older than 19, be sentenced to prison for the remainder of his or her life. Furthermore, the defendant would not be permitted to plead guilty to a lesser charge, nor be eligible for probation or parole. These statutes became known as the Rockefeller Drug Laws– a milestone in America's war on drugs. The laws almost immediately led to an increase in drug convictions, but no measurable decrease in overall crime. Black people began going to prison in droves. Dr. King probably turned over in his grave."

"Sounds like the beginnings of the war on terror," he said.

At that point for some reason, the dates Reverend Milton had given me years ago popped into my mind. Rockefeller's drug law was introduced in New York in

1973. Imbler v. Pachman was decided in 1976. Reagan signed the Anti-Drug Abuse Act, the act that made Rockefeller's drug law national, in 1986. Nixon and Reagan were simply following Rockefeller's orders. I wondered how many members of the Imbler court had taken large fees for speaking at billionaire events. This was the shit Milton had been looking for.

"Well, sort of," I said after I swallowed hard. "It was a continuation of the war on drugs carefully planned and orchestrated in the early 1900s by John D. Junior to protect the family ownership of a chemically-based pharmaceutical monopoly. It was also the beginning of the school-to-prison pipeline, the same pipeline that has resulted in thousands of Black men being sent to prison."

We said our goodbyes for a second time, and hung up. Sitting there, staring at the phone, my mood was completely different. The self-confidence I had felt at the beginning of the call was tempered by the enormity of the problem. I wondered what I would do if I were president. I wondered what my options would be. As commander in chief of one of the strongest armies in the world, I would think I had lots of options. I wondered how much planning it would take for the armed forces to capture all the personnel and assets of all twelve federal reserve banks. Then I wondered what it would take to coordinate that effort with England, Russia, France, Germany, all the countries that had a Rothschild-Rockefeller central banking system. It would take a president with balls to even imagine such a venture, let alone begin to implement it. Presidents these days don't have balls like that. Maybe they remembered what happened to Kennedy.

I decided to stick to our original plan of killing billionaires one by one along with their families.

I dismantled the phone Menachem had sent me. I crushed the chip that was in it. I placed the pieces in a plastic bag that I would take with me on my next trip outside, and distribute the pieces around the neighborhood in various garbage cans and sewer openings.

I felt good. I felt confident. It would take time, maybe years, but I knew the plan would work. My target was going to be the Cack twins, Davin and Chauncey Cack.

They say Marie Antoinette uttered the words, 'Let them eat cake.' Who said them isn't important. What is important is the expression of contempt for the masses those words conveyed. It is also said that those words cost her her head.

Similar words have been uttered in this epoch. In mocking the Occupy Wall Street movement, the first of the Cack twins, Davin, founded a movement of his own which he coined Occupy Waldorf. At least he claims to have coined the name. He founded his movement in response to the Citigroup Plutonomy Report dated March 5, 2006, which warned of possible push-back from the poor to the increasing wealth of the rich.

The report warned that the poor, through the concept of one person, one vote, could derail the gravy train the rich have been riding for the last 30 years. Davin Cack's plan was to suppress voter registration nationwide in order to undercut the power of the poor to challenge the power of the rich.

According to the report, "this could be felt through higher taxation (on the rich or indirectly though higher corporate taxes/regulation) or through trying to protect indigenous laborers, in a push-back on globalization – either anti-immigration, or protectionism." To prevent these kinds of push-backs, Davin planned to prevent poor people from voting.

The other twin, Chauncey Cack, claimed that God made him rich, and that he was entitled to his riches. Well, Asshole, God made me an assassin. Let's see how that works out for you and your brother. Like Marie Antoinette, the words you utter might cost you your head. If you want to go to the party, you got to dance with the one what brung you. It was time for the Cacks to pay the piper. Humanity was coming to collect, and I was their spokesman.

I put the bag with the phone parts on the floor by the kitchen table. Then I piled all the dwarf's belongings on the table, a passport, a purse with loose change, documents from a rental car company, the box cutter.

I opened the passport. His name was Dietger Scheermann. According to his passport, he was a U.S. citizen. And judging from the stamps in it, he had spent a lot of time traveling the world. This book was not even five years old, and it was already nearly full. I flipped to the last page. It had an Israeli stamp on it. He had been in Israel at the same time I was! Could he have been the one passing out literature in Caesarea?

I replaced the passport and picked up the rental car documents. He'd had this car for a while. Maybe because he'd made all those modifications to it so he could drive it. There was the contract itself, some insurance waivers, and something else. It was a pink sheet folded up and stuck between the contract and the waiver. I unfolded it. It was a receipt from a nursing home over on Lawrence Avenue. It was for an Annie Miller.

It couldn't be! Could Mighty Red still be alive? The

image of her striding forward with those huge tits came to my mind. Thinking back on it, she was probably 20 or 30 years older than me. That would make her what? 80? 90? 95 maybe? I needed to see.

I took the picture from one of the passports Menachem gave to me, and put it over the picture in Deitger's passport. It was crude, but I wanted to have something in case the nursing home had a list of people who could visit. I wanted to already be on the list.

I went by the next morning. It was cold, but the snow had stopped. It had dumped about a foot on us. The main streets were plowed. The city was working on the side streets. The day was bright and sunny and cold. There were mounds of snow with cars under them. I was glad I had a parking space right in the building that led out onto a plowed road. The screen on my smart phone said it was 10 degrees.

The nursing home had a parking lot that was already clear. That made it easy. Not many people came visiting that day because of the snow drifts. Lots of would-be visitors were probably digging out.

The guard at the front desk asked for my name when I told him I was there to see Annie Miller. I told him my name was Sherman. He checked his list, and let me in. I didn't even need the fake passport.

"I think I've seen your picture on her little table," he said.

"Could you check which room she's in?" I asked. "The last time I was here, they had moved her."

The guard gave me the room number. It was to the right down the main hallway. The room was on the left. The door was open.

Not knowing quite what to expect, I peeked in first. It was a double-occupancy room, but only one bed was being used. The pale grey curtain separating the beds was pushed all the way over to the pastel green wall. The room smelled of pine cleaner. The lone occupant sat in a wheelchair by the window gazing out over the glistening white snow.

I stepped in and approached her. I stopped by the first bed. Her's was the one closest to the window. There was a small table on the other side of her bed in the corner under the window. It had an unlit candle and something under a purple satin handkerchief. The woman in the wheelchair turned her head slowly to look at me.

Her hair was white. Her skin was pasty white, and sagged more on one side of her face than on the other. There were bluish bags under her eyes. Her gown was white and stained with something she had eaten for breakfast. Strawberry jam. Ketchup. Something reddish. Maybe it was a medication she was taking, some kind of red syrup. It was her. Anna Müller. Those huge tits were shriveled now, and sagged down to her waist.

I chuckled at the irony. Mighty Red looked all white. And, seeing me, had the blues. Her expression was priceless. She had clearly at some point had a stroke. Spit ran out of the left corner of her mouth. She held her left hand in a fist, and kept in resting in her lap. Only her right eye widened as she recognized who I was. The right side of her mouth opened. A sound came out, but it wasn't a word. Just a grunt.

"I missed you, Red," I taunted as I sat on the side of her bed. "Did you miss me?"

She began to shiver. I couldn't tell if she was cold or nervous or afraid or pissed-off or what. Her head began to oscillate from side to side as if she were signaling no very quickly and surreptitiously.

"Dietger is dead," I told her.

She moaned again, only this time it was plaintive. Her head rocked back still shaking no. Her legs began to twitch.

"He tried to kill me again. I had to defend myself." I paused for a moment, then asked, "Did you order him to shoot me back then?"

Now she was afraid. Maybe she thought– or at least

had hoped– I would not remember that part. She pulled her head back upright, and looked around the room. Her gaze stopped on the table with the purple satin handkerchief.

"What have you got there, Red?" I asked.

I reached over and snatched the purple cloth from its place. A white mannequin's hand lay underneath. It had been completely hidden. Beneath that, a small stick-doll lay on its back. The mannequin's hand had been holding the stick doll in place. There was a pin stuck in its side in the same place that I had been shot in my side. Underneath the doll, there was a picture of me in my Air Force uniform. I was about to ask where she got it, but then I remembered. Ruby must have given it to her. I looked over at her, and the little miniature no oscillations had changed into little miniature yes oscillations. She obviously had no control over her head. She was riveted with fear. Her head twitched. Her legs twitched. The hand she held in a fist twitched.

"I'm not going to kill you," I said. "I want you to live to see what I am about to do in the world."

She seemed unpersuaded. None of the twitching stopped.

"You got a TV?"

I looked around the room for one. There was none.

"Tell these folks you need a TV. I want you to be able to see the news. The people you serve are about to start dying."

I reached over and took the mannequin's hand from off the stick doll and dropped it into the wicker waste basket sitting beside the table. I picked the doll up, and removed the pin from its side. Oddly, my side felt better. The scar I had there felt less tight. I stuffed the doll into my pocket.

"You won't be needing this any more," I said.

I took the picture of me, and put that into the same pocket. I stood up preparing to leave. Just then, a thought occurred to me.

"Dietger became a U.S. citizen," I said. "Did you? And did you use Annie Miller on the application? Or did you use Anna Müller? You know that lying on a citizenship application is a serious matter, especially for a Nazi war criminal."

The thought of deportation was so sobering, she stopped twitching.

"I wouldn't worry too much about that, though," I said. "You're old and weak. They will probably have mercy on you."

I chortled as I turned and left the room.

XXIII

"Can I come to your house?" Jiqin asked.

"I don't know if that's a good idea," I answered.

"Do you have a woman?"

"The last one I had burned the house down."

I didn't want to have to explain the blood lust I had been experiencing lately, so I didn't bother mentioning Brit. I could see Brit's face, though. And I could see the ways in which she and Kelly were similar. They had the same shallow cheeks, the same thick nose and lips, the same crescent hairline.

"I've already apologized," Jiqin said. "It's time for me-- for *us*-- to move on."

I needed time to think about it. I needed to consider whether or not I wanted to take a chance on being so deeply hurt again. By the same token, I did miss her.

"Just for tonight," I said. "Just for tonight."

Because the battery in my garage door opener suddenly died, I parked around the corner from the house. Jiqin and I walked slowly back to the front of the building. The air was crisp and cold. I breathed it in deeply thinking about what Jiqin coming back into my life could mean. It crossed my mind that she might be exactly who I needed right now. So I asked her, "How's your crew?"

"They're all dead now."

"Have you gotten out of the business?"

"It's been years," she answered. Then she asked, "Why?"

"I was just wondering," I said.

"Yes," she said, "I'm out of the business."

"And I guess your uncle is dead," I ventured.

"Yes. He's been dead for some years," she said. "Why are you asking about those times? They're gone, all gone."

"He wasn't that old."

"No, he wasn't," she said. "But he got sick."

"SARS?" I asked.

"Yes! How did you know?"

Just then, I thought I saw a shadow by one of the hedges off to one side of the building. But I was tired. I could have been seeing anything.

"Maybe we need to bring those times back," I said. "Do you have any contacts?"

"Not here," she answered. "They're all back in China. Why? What do you have in mind?"

"There are some people who need to die."

"There are always people who need to die," she said. "Who in particular?"

"I'm still working on that part. But it'll be a billionaire."

"Who's going to finance it?"

"This is strictly public service."

"Murder is not public service," she said.

"In this case," I said, "it is."

"Why billionaires?" she asked.

"Because they're billionaires."

"That's it?"

"Well," I said, "yes. That's it."

"How many billionaires do you plan to hit?"

"All of them."

"And their families?"

"Yeah, them too."

The traffic on Sheridan Road was light. A bus crept by going south with hardly anyone on it. It was clear from her demeanor that the driver was killing time to her next stop. A motorcycle couple zoomed north in matching green and yellow body suits. The bikes scarcely make any noise. As we approached the glass front door, someone called in a loud whisper, "Daddy."

I looked to my left. It was Brit. Kelly was with her. Kelly had a coat on over her pajamas.

"Why have you got her out so late?" I asked. "This child should be in bed." I was genuinely concerned.

Brit saw Jiqin and asked, "Who's she?"

Before I could answer, Jiqin said, "I'm his wife."

"We are his family," Brit countered, hugging Kelly close to her side.

"Why didn't you tell me about her?" Jiqin asked.

"Why didn't you tell *me* about *her*?" Brit asked.

"Slow down, guys," I said. "There is a good explanation for all of this. But let's get upstairs so we can get this child to bed."

"I want to know who this bitch think she is," Brit said.

"Don't go there, Brit," I warned. "She will beat your ass worse than I will."

Jiqin took a small step back and looked away at the ground, but I could tell that Brit was still within the range of her peripheral vision. She was being humble, but taking no chances.

"How did you get this address?" I asked Brit.

"I'm a reporter," she answered. "I make it my business to find things out. We wouldn't have played the way we did without me knowing who you were and where you lived."

I wondered if she had something at her house that would have implicated me had I followed my urge to kill her. I was glad I had not done it.

Jiqin caught the reference to the life style, and picked

up on it.

"I'm not his wife," she said, "I'm his submissive."

Now Brit was interested.

"Well, I'm his sub, too," she said to Jiqin. Then to me, "I thought you didn't know what a sub was. Now you've got two of us? You're a fast learner."

"Can we talk about this upstairs?" I asked. "Kelly needs to be in bed."

As we stepped into the elevator, I could see them each sizing the other up, I suspected considering possible play sessions. I pushed the button for my floor.

We put Kelly in my bed, and closed the door. She was so tired, she didn't even ask for a story. Brit and Jiqin went into the living room. I sat in the kitchen. I could hear Brit and Jiqin making small talk.

Before long, Brit began telling Jiqin things about her life that she had never told even me. She explained that she was able to pursue her life's ambition of free-lance journalism and photography because she had years ago won a settlement in a lawsuit against the Chicago police department.

Apparently, she was driving alone one evening, and an officer stopped her for a minor traffic violation. During that encounter, the officer accused her of disobeying one of his orders. He beat her up, and to teach her a lesson she wouldn't forget, he raped her right in the back seat. At trial, he claimed their sex was consensual, but the jury didn't believe him. She wound up with enough money to buy a six unit apartment building. Income from the building allowed her to do what she wanted to do. She never told Kelly that story. That cop was Kelly's father. And clearly he was a brother, because Kelly was much darker than Brit.

Next, Brit told Jiqin about meeting me, and how we were really a good match together. This from the woman who made me jump through hoops just to move a few of my things into her apartment. She told her everything except the part about drinking piss from my dick. That part she left out.

Then Brit cut to the chase, asking the questions she really wanted to ask in the first place, but not wanting to appear to be nosy. Having told her story first, now it would be merely sharing.

"So how long have *you* known him?" she asked.

Jiqin told her the whole story. Well, almost the whole story. She omitted the part about trafficking in Mexican illegal aliens, and she certainly omitted the part about having to kill one of them.

When she got to the part about the baby dying, she cried again anew. Brit hugged her, and she told Brit about the play session she and I had to help cleanse her of her guilt.

"I needed him to fuck me to help me forgive myself for what I had done," she said.

I tried to remember what we had together, Jiqin and I. All I could remember at the moment was how quickly she had dispatched one of the men she was trafficking. His name was Juan. He had run out of money, and had hoped to scare her into letting him live at our house rent-free for a month rather than for merely a week. He pulled a knife on her, and within fewer than ten seconds, he was on the floor fatally stabbed with his own blade.

It seemed so incongruous to see the person I remembered stabbing Juan to death now in the living room crying over a dead baby. She was as cold as a stone back then. Now she was as weepy as a willow. Brit was comforting her, but it didn't seem to be enough. I scooted my chair back from the kitchen table, and made my way in to join them.

I hadn't expected my voice to sound as condescending as it did, but once it was out, I couldn't change it. I asked, "Do you need me to fuck you again?"

Because of my tone of voice, I had expected a resounding, hell no. Instead, I got a tentative maybe.

"I'll be fine," she said. Her voice betrayed a sense of

uncertainty.

"Well, if she won't take the offer, I will," Brit said. "And I want some more knife play. You had me scared to fucking death that day. Why haven't you called me?"

Her request caught me by surprise. I didn't know how to react. For sure, I didn't want to do it. I came too close to killing her last time. Next time, I might not be able to stop myself.

"How did you find out my address?" I asked.

"I told you," she said. "I'm a reporter. I know how to find shit out. I have long known where you lived. I thought you knew that."

I knew no such thing. But I didn't say that out loud.

"And I suppose you had it written somewhere in you apartment," I said.

"Of course. Why else do you think I would agree to doing knife play? I always keep myself protected," she said.

"I cannot do any more knife play," I told her. "I could feel myself coming too close to wanting to do it for real."

The expression of anticipation on Brit's face changed. The eagerness in her eyes changed to dread.

"You mean I was in real danger?" she asked.

"Yes," I answered. "I was so close."

Brit began to shiver.

"I'm getting scared all over again just thinking about it," she said. "I need you inside me."

"No," I said. "I don't want to relive that play session."

"We won't be reliving it. This will be a new and different session."

"No," I said again.

"Please. This is the last time I will feel fear this intense while playing. Let me have this."

She scooted down to the middle of the couch and climbed out of her panties. Lying on one side, she lifted her leg and spread herself.

"It won't get hard," I protested. "I just fucked Jiqin for an hour. I am not Superman."

"Yes, you are," she said. "You can do this."

She waddled off the couch, and came over to where I was sitting on the floor. She got on her knees, and unzipped my pants.

"It won't get hard," I told her again.

Not wanting to take no for an answer, she sucked on it for ten minutes to no avail. Shorty was done for the night.

While Brit and I were on the floor, Jiqin crawled up onto the couch, and fell asleep. I found some extra blankets in the linen closet and covered her up. Then Brit and I fell asleep next to each other on the living room rug.

XXIV

"I think I wet the bed."

I rolled over and looked up. Kelly was standing right at my head. It was early morning, and the light from the window filled the room with a pale glow.

"I think I wet the bed," she said again.

I nudged Brit.

"Get up, and take care of this," I told her.

I nudged Brit again. This time she reacted.

"What?" she asked.

"The baby wet the bed," I told her.

"Aw, shit! I'm sorry."

"Don't be sorry. Just get up and take care of it."

She sighed deeply, then rolled to her other side. She sat up.

"Okay," she said. "Where do you keep the clean sheets?"

I told her, and she hoisted herself up. She picked Kelly up, and walked her back into the bedroom to change the bed.

After a few minutes, she called out, "Do you have a big plastic garbage bag? The mattress got wet, and I need something to protect the other side of the bed."

"Aw, man, I don't feel like getting up to get it."

"Just tell me where it is."

"In the kitchen under the sink."

I was about to roll back over and pull the blanket up under my chin. But I saw Jiqin sitting in the chair in the corner flipping through a book, *the* book. I must have left it on the little bookshelf also in that corner.

"I recognize this picture," she said. "It's just like the picture my mother had next to the Buddha at home. I told you about that."

"Yes," I said, "I remember you telling me that."

"I told you that she was one of your children."

"*Seine Kinder*," I said.

"Yes," she said. "But you didn't tell me that it was you for real. You led me to believe that the resemblance was a coincidence."

"At the time, I didn't want to be reminded of them," I said.

"Well, what about now?"

"Now might be different," I said. "I have only recently come into the possession of that book."

"So, is it you?"

"It's my uncle," I said. "My great uncle, actually."

"So, what does it all mean?"

"I have no clue," I said, and I wasn't lying.

Jiqin shifted in her chair as the light from the window

behind her backlit her like a silhouette.

"My mother used to swoon over your picture. It's ironic that you and I have become as close as we have."

"Yes," I said, "almost as if it were preordained."

"So, what does it all mean?" she asked again, her voice wispy and trailing off.

This time, I didn't bother to answer. She wasn't really asking me anyway. She was more accurately tossing a naked question out to the ether. I didn't know if she expected an answer.

Brit came back in from changing the bed, and flopped on the couch where Jiqin had slept.

"So, are you guys up for good or what?" she asked. "'Cause I could use some more sleep."

"I could, too," I said. I pulled the blanket up around my neck, and turned over so the light from the window wouldn't keep me awake. Jiqin continued leafing through the book.

When I woke up, Brit, Kelly and Jiqin were in the kitchen making pancakes. Brit was showing Kelly how to break eggs, and Jiqin was squeezing oranges.

"You gon' sleep all morning?" Brit asked.

"I thought you needed more sleep all of a sudden," I responded.

"I did," she answered. "I slept for another hour."

Damn! That meant I must have slept for more than an hour. I got up and gathered up all the extra blankets from the living room, and stuffed them back into the linen closet. I took a short shower. When I got out, they had breakfast on the table waiting. Pancakes, scrambled eggs, orange juice, coffee. Certainly more than I would have had had they not been here. I could get used to this.

I flipped on the big screen before going into the kitchen to eat. There was a short blurb about Aba going to trial soon. Jiqin must have noticed my increased attention to that story.

"He's the one who shot the prime minister of Israel, isn't he?" she asked.

"That's him," Brit answered. "Asshole! Who would do something like that?"

Jiqin poured syrup over her pancakes as she continued to focus her attention on me. Reflexively, I looked away. Realizing that looking away was a mistake, I looked back at her, but I was too late. She widened her eyes and dipped her head just a little as if to ask, 'Was it you?' I looked away again. I knew that she knew the truth.

That's when I noticed that Kelly was looking at both of us. She was about to put a forkful of eggs into her mouth, but stopped in mid-stride. She looked at me, then at Jiqin, then back at me, then back at Jiqin. I couldn't tell whether or not she knew what we were communicating. She seemed too young to know, but she did notice that something was going on that we were not voicing. She put the forkful of eggs into her mouth, and chewed, slowly at first, then at a more normal pace. I looked back over at Jiqin. She shrugged.

I reached the syrup, and slathered it all over my pancakes. I ate a bite, then another and another. Brit was a good cook! The pancakes were light and moist. The eggs were fluffy.

About halfway through the meal, Jiqin said, "I finished that book."

"Oh?" I asked, "What did you think?"

"I think it's you. You *are* the one."

"What book?" Brit asked.

"A book I recently got from an ex-friend of mine," I said. "It's over there on the little bookcase."

"What's it about?"

"It's just a book," I said.

"He is being modest," Jiqin said. "Our Dom is the Messiah, and we are His Children."

"Yeah, right!" Brit chortled.

I hadn't thought about it before then, but Jiqin was right. I had, in a twisted kind of way, become mankind's redeemer. I tried to remember what, if anything, Lillian had told me about my great uncle, and why he had started *Seine Kinder*. I couldn't remember anything she told me.

I remembered reading a *Time* article back then that said members of a religious sect in Germany known as *Seine Kinder* claim to have witnessed the second coming of the Messiah. It was me, and I didn't even know it.

I remembered the man who had crashed his green Mercedes into the parked car the day I was heading for Frieda's place, and who told the ambulance driver that I was God. The notion was ludicrous back then. But now anything seemed possible.

Then, all at once, I could hear Lillian's voice again. "You are God," she had said. "Or rather, you look like God. More precisely, you look like the person who shortly after World War I formed a movement, a cult, who set himself up as the cult's one and only prophet, and who prophesied shortly before his death that he would return and lead his children, *Seine Kinder*, to heaven." Maybe I couldn't lead *Seine Kinder* to heaven, but I could certainly try to lead them out of the billionaire cabal's hell. And maybe that would be good enough.

We finished the meal in silence. Afterwards, I went into the living room to see if I could get any more news on

Aba. Brit and Jiqin were in the kitchen loading dishes into the dishwasher. Kelly made a beeline to the corner and began flipping through the book. She couldn't read well enough to read that book, so she was gratified to find the pictures in the middle. Then she found the picture glued in at the back. She stared at it for what seemed like a long time. Then she closed the book and ambled back into the kitchen to be with her mother.

Once the breakfast dishes were in the dishwasher and the counters all wiped, the girls came into the living room with me.

"We're leaving," Brit said. "But we'll be back tonight. We still have some unfinished business to take care of."

"I'm leaving, too," Jiqin said. "By the way, I sent a text to my contacts in China. We're putting together a new crew. We'll be open for business in about a month."

"Will you be back tonight as well?" I asked.

"Absolutely! I'm anxious to try out my new playmate."

She turned and looked at Brit. Brit giggled and put the coat on the baby.

As they were leaving, the first book of Genesis came to mind. "And God said, 'Let there be light,' and there was light." With that, I thought about Ida at the library over on 73rd and Exchange. That was the day she introduced me to Aba. I remembered what she had been holding forth about. She was explaining what she called the 'matter cycle.'

"Scientists think matter ceases to exist when it gets sucked into a black hole," she had said. "It gets squeezed so small that it goes out of existence. But that's ridicules. Black holes are where light gets converted into dark matter."

I remembered seeing Aba hanging on her every word. His choirboy face was upturned as if he were transfixed. Maybe he was. Or maybe he was faking. I wondered if he was a CIA operative back then.

"At some point in the universe," she continued, "dark matter gets converted back into light. And just as a fish cannot know where water goes when it evaporates, or where it comes from when it rains, we cannot know where matter goes when it becomes dark matter, nor where it comes from during bursts of light like supernova events. That's where 'Let there be light' comes from," she said. "That's how God separated the light from the darkness."

Maybe she was crazier than I thought.

I watched Brit and Kelly and Jiqin round the corner down the hall towards the elevators. Then I closed the door, and I locked it.

XXV

Oh, Mary Mack, Mack, Mack,
All dressed in black, black, black,
With silver buttons, buttons, buttons,
All down her back, back, back.

I liked playing double Dutch with the girls. I was about twelve. I wasn't any good at it, but there was something about watching them bounce in unison as they turned the ropes, as they timed their movements just before entering the whirling lines.

Sometimes, the big girls would join in. They would gather their dress bottoms into a wad at the middle of their thighs, and hold it there until they jumped in and finally missed. And all the girls had different jumping styles. Some would jump on two feet. Others would jump on alternating feet. Some would use both styles, first one, then the other. They always jumped on one foot twice as they turned to face the opposite direction. I never understood why. The ones that were good could jump out again without being touched. It was like a ballet played out in one-two time.

They all knew I couldn't jump, but the game always took a different tenor when I was around. They would get giggly, and I would pretend to be better than I actually was.

One day, one of the big girls, her name was Sadie, joined in the play. She was a comely girl, all of about 15 years old. She had dark eyes and a wide nose and thick lips. She always licked them as she bounced with the rhythm getting ready to jump in. This time as she jumped in, her blouse came unbuttoned. She didn't seem to notice, but I was hypnotized. The top button came undone. Then the button below that. But she was busy holding onto that wad of skirt, so she didn't notice. Her blouse was open half way down to her navel. Then she jumped high enough to allow the rope to go beneath her twice rather than the customary once, and upon landing, one of her tits flopped out of her bra. It was dark and full and supple. She jumped twice more, then stopped abruptly, dropped her skirt, and clutched her chest. She covered herself and re-buttoned her blouse. Then she sat on the stoop of the building we were in front of.

The other girls gave me a sly, knowing half-look. They would look at me briefly, then look away. I thought I could see a half-smile on some of them. I never did figure out what was happening. The other girls tried to restart the game, but it was forced. The flow was gone. I tried to get Sadie to rejoin us, but she was embarrassed, or so it seemed.

After a while, I left.

I would see them jumping several times in the following days, but Sadie was never there. I would watch them from a distance, but I never joined in again. The truth was that I only liked playing double Dutch with the girls because I liked being close to Sadie. When she wasn't there, I had no interest in the game.

She asked her mother, mother, mother,
For 15 cents, cents, cents,
To see the elephant, elephant, elephant,
Jump the fence, fence, fence.

I hadn't been to Bongo Beach in years. The only reason I was there tonight was because I was pissed with Brit and Jiqin, and I wanted to get out of the house in order to cool off. We all lived in my condo now, and sometimes I just needed to be alone. I had driven up and down the length of Lake Shore Drive, but it was still too early to go back home. So I stopped by the Beach to hear some music. It was only a few of miles from the house.

Folks called it Bongo Beach, because brothers, amateurs mostly, gathered there evenings during the warm months to play drums, congas usually, but some cow bells, claves and other assorted percussions as well. Once in a while, there would actually be someone there with a set of bongos. This night was warm and clear.

The number of drummers who showed up from one night to the next varied. Tonight, there was a crowd. There must have been a dozen congas out there, all competing to be heard, showing off with flashes of percussive genius, hands blazing in the light of the overhead street lamps. Some played with their eyes closed as if in meditation. Others watched their fellow musicians for tips on technique. Still others played as they flirted with the cuties in the crowd standing around the drummers, swaying to the music.

My favorite was an older brother wearing no shirt and cut-off jeans. His sandals and feet were worn and covered with dust and sand from the beach. He had sticks of burning incense wedged under the ring that held the drum head in place. He was one of the ones who played with his eyes closed. His drum was old, the mahogany finish worn and chipped, but his technique was flawless. It almost sounded as if his rhythm was carrying the ensemble. When he changed, they changed. He was the master.

Tonight, he was in especially high form. And it seemed

incongruous, because tonight his nose was broken. He wore one of those bandages on it to hold it in place while it healed. I knew it was my imagination, but it almost seemed as if having his nose repaired gave him renewed strength. He played with a determination that demonstrated that nothing in the world could stop him. He knew with every fiber of his being that his music was going to change the planet, one soul at a time.

Sitting on a blanket in the shadow of a bush behind him, I could see a figure weaving to and fro to the music. She wore an African head wrap and a long African-print dress, yellow mostly, with splotches of orange and green. Looking closer, I could see that she was nursing a baby. That's why she was sitting in that shadow. But her breast was visible, dark and full and supple. I couldn't believe it was possible that I would see her out here for the first time since that day jumping double Dutch. I moved closer careful not to appear to be leering. But sure enough, there she was. Sadie.

The truth is, life was strange and unpredictable. The impossible could happen at any time, when you least expect it, or when you didn't expect it at all.

He jumped so high, high, high,
He touched the sky, sky, sky,

And he didn't come back, back, back,
'Til the fourth of July, -ly, -ly.

Listening to the music, I felt better. I felt rejuvenated in the soul. Drums have that power. I took a deep breath, and looked up at the sky. There were too many street lights to see many stars, but I imagined that I could sense the magnitude of the universe from where I stood. Somehow, sensing the bigger picture helped me center deeper into the mood the drums had put me in. I looked over at Sadie again. She was finished nursing the baby, and was holding it over her left shoulder patting it on the back.

I was tempted to say something to her. The problem with that was that I would have to talk. Somehow I had the feeling that talking would break my mood. Besides, she probably would not remember me anyway. Instead, I decided to head home. I eased my way through the people gathered around the drums. Everyone was bouncing and swaying to the music. I could smell their bodies, their funk and cologne. Somebody had a pachouli incense stick burning. Somebody else fired up a joint. It felt so 1960s. I thought about Milton. With him might have been the last time I had gotten high. I remembered the boats weaving in Montrose Harbor.

Where was Milton, anyway? Now that I knew some of the answers he had been looking for, maybe I could help him reach some peace, some closure. I remembered that it always bothered him that he could never figure out who was systematically thinning the ranks of Black people on the planet. I wondered if he could have himself been a Mason. I shook my head, no. Milton wasn't a joiner.

I needed to look for him, but I had no idea where to begin. The Salvation Army was no longer in the location where I had first met him, north Clark Street. The last time I thought about looking for Milton, I checked on-line for Salvation Army locations, but it seemed pointless. They were all over the map, and he could be at any one of them, or at none of them at all. I had no way of knowing. I had to resign myself to never seeing him again in this life.

Leaving the Bongo Beach parking lot, I remembered that Rainbow Beach was only a couple of miles from here. I'd heard that a criminal cannot resist the urge to return to the scene of his crime. They were right. I had to see the spot where Dietger landed like a rock.

I drove south on South Shore Drive, then turned left at 79th Street into the park. I wound slowly around to the parking lot, but there was nothing to see. The lot was crowded with cars. A red Jeep was parked where Dietger had lain.

I found a parking space and eased into it. I got out and strolled over to the tree, my tree, the one I had been under the day Dietger shot me. I sat under it again the way I had that day so many years ago. I looked out over the lake, dark and seemingly infinite. The horizon was invisible in the darkness. I looked back up at the sky hoping to deepen the feeling I had gotten at Bongo Beach. It was gone. The feeling was gone. I looked over at the ground where I had slumped, where Jiqin had come and saved me. She was young and cute back then. Maybe I was, too. I certainly had more hair back then. I remembered how Jiqin had her mouth on my mouth, blowing her life into my lungs. Her saving my life was how we had first met. I remembered feeling the pain in my side and flinching. Jiqin had raised up and looked at me. She seemed pleasantly surprised to see me.

"Don't die," she had said. "I'll call a doctor."

"No doctor," I had protested. "No doctor."

"You need a doctor!"

"It's okay if I die. I don't want a doctor."

I looked up at the branches I had felt myself drift through as I had experienced one of many out-of-body episodes I had back then. I guess I had hoped for some kind of closure from remembering that day, some kind of burst of knowledge about the universe and why things happen the way they did, and why I was who I was and why I was where I was. But nothing happened. There was no burst of knowledge, no closure, no sudden revelation of the truth. The best I could come up with was, shit happened because it happened. That was the way it had always been, and that was likely the way would always be.

I uncrossed my legs and hopped up and headed back to the car.

Oh, Mary Mack, Mack, Mack,
All dressed in black, black, black,
With silver buttons, buttons, buttons,
All down her back, back, back.

XXVI

It had been months since I had received a tell-tale box from Menachem. So when I got one yesterday, I was surprised. I knew to expect a call from him soon. When the phone rang, my curiosity was piqued.

"Hey, man," I said, "What's up?"

"I just got some interesting news," he replied.

"Oh," I answered, "What's that?"

"By the way, how is your campaign to kill the Cacks coming?"

"Quite well, actually. I've got a crew, and we're making our final plans." I asked, "What's your news?"

"I think we have an unexpected ally."

"Oh! Who?"

"Russia," he said. "More exactly, Vladimir Putin."

I had not expected that answer. And having heard it, I was unsure of what to make of it.

"Okay," I said. I tried to keep my tone of voice unrevealing, but I'm sure he was able to read something into it.

"Putin is doing what Obama dares not."

"To wit?"

"He is challenging the Rothschilds hold on the Russian economy."

Silly me! I had thought he was going to say something that was patently obvious to understand. My silence must have been his clue that it wasn't.

"Ever heard of Bank Rossiya?"

"No. Should I have?"

"Probably not," he answered. "But that is where Putin is putting all of Russia's money these days."

My response was, "So what?"

"So what, indeed," he replied. "Here's the history. The U.S. and Russia were once allies. It was Russia that protected the U.S. from Great Britain and France who, at the Rothschild's urging, were preparing to support the Confederacy during the American Civil War. You remember Lincoln's dealings with the Rothschilds, right?"

"Yes, I remember."

"Well, like Lincoln," he continued, "the Tzars of Russia had also long defied the Rothschild's attempts to hobble Russia with debt the way they had hobbled all the royalty of Europe."

"Are you going somewhere with this?" I asked.

"Yes," he answered. "Just bear with me. During the Russo-Japanese War, the Rothschild clan, through their minion, Jacob Schiff, prevented Russia from getting the funds it needed to prosecute that war. As a result, Russia suffered a humiliating defeat. This was also during the time of the first Russian revolution caused by the Rothschild-generated money market contraction of 1899 and 1900."

"There was a Russian revolution in 1900?" I asked. I had never heard about it. Or if I had, I didn't remember.

"Well," he answered, "it didn't really start until Bloody Sunday, January 22, 1905. But the climate for revolution was created by that money market contraction. Several years later, the Rothschild clan supported the Bolsheviks. As you know, this led to the second Russian revolution in 1917, and the death of Nicholas II and his entire family."

"Yes," I said, "that one I know about."

"It was no coincidence that Nicholas's brother, Michael, was murdered one month earlier," he said, "and after that second revolution, with all the Romanovs now dead, the Rothschilds established a banking foothold in Russia that remains to this day."

"Are we there, yet?"

"Yes," he answered, "enter Vladimir Putin." He paused as if to allow the name to make its full impact. Then he said, "Enter Bank Rossiya." He paused again.

I knew he wanted me to connect the dots. But at first, it wasn't happening. Then, all at once, it became clear.

"He's setting up a new Bank of Russia," I said,

"independent of the Rothschilds."

"Bingo! Give that man a cupie doll. Russia is once again asserting itself in the world of finance. Putin is laying the groundwork to do what Alexander II did in Russia years earlier, free the serfs. And unlike Obama, he doesn't have to worry about his intelligence service turning against him the way the CIA turned against Kennedy. Remember, it was the CIA's Secret Team that orchestrated Kennedy's death. But Putin used to be head of the KGB. So they won't likely attack him."

"Yes," I said, "I remember."

"And just to show you how things happen, Putin probably took his lead from Presidents Hugo Chávez and Néstor Kirchner who came up with the idea of the Bank of the South back in 2006. In fact, the reason Hugo Chávez is vilified and the U.S. Congress put sanctions on Venezuela is not because he was a socialist, but because he dared to challenge the power of the banksters. And the U.S. Congress is planning sanctions on Russia for the exact same reason. The Rothschilds are ruthless when it comes to keeping control of the world money supply."

"I think the billionaire cabal is planning another 1973," I said. "1973 was a banner year."

"Do you know why they picked 1973?"

"They picked it? It didn't just happen that way?"

"No way," Menachem said. "1973 was planned, because the numbers of that year embody 9-11. There is the '9' in the '19,' and the rest of the numbers, the 7, the 3 and the 1, add up to 11."

"That's creepy!"

"I know, but look at the history. It was September 11, 1990, when the first President Bush made that announcement about the New World Order. It was September 11, 2001, under the second President Bush when the World Trade Center towers were demolished. The numbers 9 and 11 are important to these clowns."

"Daddy Bush is a punk," I said. "Nothing more than a tool and a flunky for the billionaire cabal."

"Little George was just as bad or worse," he replied, "but Jeb is the one we need to watch."

"Why?" I asked.

"Because the real struggle is yet to come," he answered. "Remember this, the Bushes didn't win their elections. The elections were stolen on their behalf specifically so that they could execute the plan of the billionaire cabal."

"There's more to be done than what has already been done?"

"Oh, yes. There are two major constructions under way in your country right now. The first is the multilevel bunker under the Denver International Airport. The second is the Utah Data Center. In 2016, after Jeb Bush or whatever Republican candidate is elected president– or rather, after that election is stolen on his behalf– the plan will become clear. The year will be 2018. Notice that the 8 and 1 equal 9, and adding the 2 equals 11. On September 11 of 2018, the billionaire cabal will make its move to overtly enslave mankind. The operation will take place in the Denver bunker, and the information stored on the chips implanted in those of us who survive will be processed at the Utah Data Center."

"They'll have to implant billions of us," I said.

"By then," he said, "there won't be billions, only millions."

"Meaning?"

"The war to reduce the population is already under way. It was SARS in China. Now it is ebola in Africa. Both of these were manufactured to reduce the non-white population worldwide. And don't forget about AIDS."

"But they're not working," I said, "not in the numbers that would reduce the population." I remembered Jiqin telling me that Master Yuen, himself a medical doctor, had died of SARS.

"Not yet," he answered. "But give ebola time. After a large portion of the African populace has been killed off, the cure will be publicized."

"Let me guess. The cure is already out there somewhere."

"Yes, it is. Nano-silver, 10 parts per million. Cures ebola. But that information, and certainly the medication itself, is being withheld from the African market."

"And SARS?"

"It's being re-engineered as we speak," he asserted. "Fear not. It will return deadlier than ever." He paused, then asked, "What do you know about psychotronic weapons?"

"Psychotronic what?"

"Psychotronic weapons."

"Never heard of them," I said. I wasn't sure psychotronic was even a word.

"Psychotronic weapons are microwave transmissions that directly affect the human nervous system," he said.

"And do what? Make you twitch?" I thought I was being funny. I remembered Annie Miller twitching when I told her about Dietger being dead. I wondered if that was the way psychotronic weapons would make you twitch.

"No," he said, "they transmit thoughts and emotions directly into a person or crowd of people."

"So they can tell you what to do without you knowing

you've been told?"

"Exactly. It is direct mind control of the masses." Then he said, "In 1976, Zbygniew Brzezinski predicted that an elite group will take advantage of persisting social crises to use, and I quote, 'the latest modern techniques for influencing public behavior and keeping society under close surveillance and control.'" He paused again, then asked, "Who do you suppose that elite group is?"

"A wild guess," I said, "the billionaire cabal."

"That man just won another cupie doll. The billionaire cabal is, as we speak, bankrolling the California companies that are perfecting these gadgets." Then he asked, "And what do you suppose he meant by 'persisting social crises?'"

"Crowds in the streets protesting cops killing young Black men," I answered. "They knew we would do what we're doing, and they already have their plan in place to take away more freedoms."

"Bingo again. And the techniques for influencing public behavior and keeping society under control?"

"Microwave mind control," I answered.

"Now you know what I know," he said, "Now you know what I know."

I found it hard to believe that these plans that seem so obvious now have been hidden in plain view for so long.

I thought about Reverend Milton and his search for the hidden hand. He knew it was there. I remembered him calling it the King Alfred Plan. He just didn't know who it was. The billionaire cabal and their flunkies, Nixon, Kissinger, the Bushes. The list goes on and on. They are the hidden hand.

"First the Bush, then the shrub. Now the sprig?" I chortled.

"Don't laugh," he said. "Beware the sprig! The sprig is going to close it out. Using the implants and mind control technology, the billionaire cabal plans to have the sprig hobble humanity for centuries."

"He's a punk," I said, "just like his damn daddy!"

"Yes, but he has big money behind him. And big money runs America. That's why we're doing what we're doing, remember?"

I knew he was right. Another Bush in the White House could cripple the country, indeed, the planet, forever. But then, that was the billionaire cabal's plan, wasn't it? World domination? Who was it who said that one world government was coming whether we liked it or not? Oh, yeah! That would be James Warburg, son of the asshole who drafted the bill that saddled America with the Federal Reserve Bank. In his mind, and he said as much before the U.S. Senate Committee on Foreign Relations on

February 17, 1950, the only question was whether World Government would be achieved by conquest or consent.

"And think about this," Menachem continued, "the sprig or whoever would be the 45th president of the United States."

"Yeah, and?"

"4 and 5 equals 9," he answered.

"Oh, I see. The sprig being number 9 makes him worse than the other two."

"In their minds, better than the other two. His being a number 9 makes him special, and a lot more dangerous for us."

My mind was buzzing. I needed to think. I wanted to close out this conversation, but couldn't think of a graceful way to do it. Finally, I just blurted out, "Listen, man, I got to go."

The conversation on the phone was over, but it was not over in my head. I couldn't stop pondering what more Jeb Bush could do to fuck the country up. I kept hearing his daddy repeating the phrase, 'And we will,' from his September 11, 1990, speech. Clearly, the billionaire cabal had the perfect minions in the members of the Bush clan. Some folks would do anything for the privilege of sucking a rich prick's dick.

I removed the chip from the phone, and broke it. I

dropped the pieces down the toilet.

"You okay, daddy?" Brit asked, having heard the toilet flush.

"I'm straight," I replied.

"I hope you know we are still in here waiting for you," Jiqin said.

"Start without me," I said. "I need to recheck our game plan."

"The game plan is fine," Jiqin said. "Brit and I checked it while you were on the phone."

"And the guys are ready?" I asked. "We strike tomorrow, you know."

"Yes, I know, and they're ready to die if they have to."

"We could all die," I said. "This has got to work. It is time for the truth to finally come to light. Corporations and the billionaire families that own and run them are, and maybe always have been, more powerful than all the governments of the world."

"You are preaching to the choir," Jiqin said.

I couldn't stop myself. I continued on as if to convince them, but I was really trying to convince myself.

"This strike against the Cach twins tomorrow will be the first in a string of billionaire killings to bring them to justice," I said. "We have got to make this work. We are going to bite the hidden hand. Bit by bit and bite by bite, we are going to bite the hidden hand off!"

"I know, right?" Brit chimed in. "But I'm doing it for the Panthers, especially those still in prison. They started it. We're going to finish it."

The doubt I was feeling gnawed at me. I could feel my stomach begin to churn. My mouth felt dry. "I just hope we're ready," I said.

"We're on it," Jiqin said, "and if we don't get them tomorrow, we will hunt them down until we do. If it takes a month, a year, ten years, the Cach twins are going to die."

"This will be the first step towards rescuing mankind," I said, "making mankind free again in a way that it has not been in hundreds of years, and maybe ever."

"We're on it," Jiqin said again. "We're on it. So for now, take your clothes off and let's fuck."

I reached down and unzipped my pants. Brit came over and pulled them off for me. She put scented oil on my feet. I think it was calendula oil. I was reminded of that day in the back of her truck when she first sucked my dick. She was different now. Or rather, her hair was different. She now wore it in a 'fro gathered at the top of her head like a crown or sweet potato pie, the roots glistening grey like diamonds against her dark chocolate skin. I leaned back on the bed as she took me into her mouth. Jiqin straddled my face with her pussy in *my* mouth. I sucked her and she came at the same time Brit came from sucking me. The scent of the two of them made my head swoon. I was truly in the garden of earthly delights, but all I could do was doubt. I had doubts about whether this plan would work.

I had Brit lie on her back. Then I had Jiqin lie on top of her stomach to stomach. I scooted between their legs, and entered Brit for a few strokes. Then I entered Jiqin for a few strokes. Then back to Brit, then back to Jiqin. I was in heaven, but I couldn't enjoy it. I didn't want any of my people to die tomorrow. If they did, I didn't want their sacrifice to be in vain. I so wanted this hit to work, I sobbed like a child. I rolled off them to one side of the bed, and I cried.

About the author

Larry Redmond is a writer, photographer and attorney. He attended the University of Illinois at Chicago, where he majored in Philosophy and minored in English. He later attended the John Marshall Law School, earning a Juris Doctor degree. He formerly worked as a criminal defense attorney representing high-profile death row inmates, several of whom were released pursuant to DNA testing. He now litigates civil rights cases in federal court. He is a member of the National Lawyers Guild.

Larry Redmond is a member of the Perspectivists writers collective, the oldest continuously active writers' workshop in Chicago.

He studied Art and Photography at Chicago State University, and became a member of the Chicago Alliance of African-American Photographers. He is a past member of the Washington Park Camera Club, one of the oldest continuously running camera clubs in Chicago.

He has seven children and three grandchildren. His hobbies include yoga and meditation.

He currently works and lives with his family in Chicago, Illinois.

Visit Penknife Press, the quill that can gut you, on-line at
www.penknifepress.com.

www.ingramcontent.com/pod-product-compliance
Lightning Source LLC
Chambersburg PA
CBHW021500240626
47154CB00002B/453